MEDITERRANEAN SUNSET

YVETTE CANOURA

Mediterranean Sunset

Yvette Canoura

Second edition: 2021

©Yvette Canoura 2019

www.yvettecanoura.com

ISBN 978-1-7349980-0-9

Ibrahim, you are the love of my life,
my fountain of inspiration, my best friend, and my soul mate.

Hasan, you are the most precious gift God has ever given me.

Prologue

"I haven't spoken to you in a while, is everything all right?" Esmaa asked.

"Things couldn't be better, my darling Esmaa. How do you like your new living arrangements?" Fouad asked.

"I'm bored without you. I need to see you."

"Patience, my dear. We've only been apart for a few months."

"It seems like an eternity."

"Rome wasn't built in a day. It might be years until our next encounter."

"Years? I can't stand being another minute without you!" Esmaa struggled to keep from sounding desperate.

"I miss your feistiness my dear, but we have to stick to our plan. You know what's at stake. We have a lot to do before we can move ahead. In the meantime, I will cherish our unforgettable goodbye."

"A man like you has needs. You can't stay faithful for long," Esmaa complained.

"Who said anything about faithful? We have an agreement and you know the rules. You establish yourself in the United States; I keep going on with my life in Antarah, as planned, and when it's time, I'll send for you."

"Aren't you afraid that I might meet someone who will sweep me off my feet and you'll lose me forever?"

"I don't think that's going to happen, but in the event it does, I might have to arrange a surprise visit to make you disappear. However, I'm certain that won't be necessary."

"You are so full of yourself," she nagged.

"And you are so turned on by it," he countered. "Just stay focused on the goal and we will be together sooner than you can imagine. Remember, do not call me. I will keep in touch."

"I love you," Esmaa said as Fouad hung up. The click of the receiver echoed in her ear. As Esmaa fought back tears, her friend, Diana, walked in.

"What's wrong Esmaa? Have you been crying?" she asked concerned.

"Don't be silly. Just allergies. My life couldn't be better. No commitments, months away from graduating, a dream job at NASA. What else can I ask for?"

"Indeed, you are a very lucky girl," Diana admitted.

"Luck has nothing to do with it," Esmaa remarked. "I work hard; I'm intelligent, possess certain attributes, and know how to use them to my advantage. I always get what I want."

"Add modesty to your list," Diana said as she assessed Esmaa and admitted that she was striking; not beautiful in the traditional sense of the word, but alluring in a self- confident, self-possessed way.

"I'd love to stay and chat but I have a meeting with Dr. Lorenz. I'll see you later."

Esmaa breezed past Diana on her way out of the apartment, leaving her signature scent of sandalwood and vanilla.

chapter 1

My Meeting with Destiny

My fate was sealed before I was even conceived. No one knew it at the time, but I was destined to live a life filled with grief. Although many people think that we can change our destinies, the Muslim faith believes that Allah has mapped out our lives from birth to death. Therefore, our path has to be accepted as God's will.

As I sat in silence gazing out the window of the limousine, I suddenly became aware that we were turning into the driveway of a large two story mansion.

Although it was dark, the reflection from the headlights made it apparent that the grounds were covered with beautiful plush gardens.

"Welcome to our home, Fatima," Fouad said. "I'm sure that you will be pleased with our new life here."

As we pulled up to the front door, I slowly stepped out of the limo and looked around. I realized at that moment that I could never warm up to a house that was as cold as my feelings towards my new husband.

"Come back for us in the morning," Fouad told the driver as he closed the door.

There was no escaping my fate now. My nightmare was about to begin and there was no way out of this irrational dilemma my father had put me in.

As we entered, the smell of tobacco permeated the entire room. Fouad proudly led me through the beautifully decorated house. When we finally reached the backyard, I was surprised and for a brief moment happy to see a lap pool.

I drifted off to my childhood remembering the countless hours I spent in the pool training for the swim team. In the beginning, my father disapproved because in Islam it is haraam, a sin, for a woman to exhibit herself in a bathing suit. Nevertheless, Mama convinced him to let me continue and, like any proud parent, he was thrilled when I brought home a trophy after a swim meet.

"I had it built especially for you," he said. "Your father told me that you are an avid swimmer."

Suddenly, he started rubbing my shoulders as he continued to talk. Chills ran down my spine. "I hope this will be an incentive for you to always keep your body as perfect and inviting as it is right now."

Slowly pulling away, I looked up to see him staring at me like a vulture that had just spotted its prey.

We continued walking through the house and came to a staircase that went to the second floor. Fouad suddenly grabbed my hand tightly and led me up the steps. Even though there was more to see, Fouad seemed uninterested at this point in showing me the rest of the house. He had other plans.

"I've saved the best for last," he said. "Our bedroom."

We entered a room that was spacious with deep burgundy walls and oversized mahogany furniture with gold detail. Fouad walked over to the large custom made bed and sat down.

"Here," he said patting the mattress, "is where we will consummate our marriage tonight."

My stomach was in knots.

He got up, closed the door, and proceeded to unloosen his tie and unbutton his shirt. As I watched him unbuckle his belt, I felt ill.

He sat in a huge, plush chair and kicked off his shoes. He looked like a king on his throne waiting for me to throw myself at his feet. He reached over and poured himself a Scotch as he looked at me intently.

"So, are you just going to stand there?" he asked.

I did not know what to say.

"You are aware that it is our wedding night. Take off all that jewelry except for the pieces I gave you," he insisted.

I followed his instructions. It took about five minutes to remove all of the gold. He stood up and helped me with the clasps on the chains. He also unzipped my dress. Then, he sat back down in the chair.

"Show me what's under the clothes," he ordered.

"You want me to undress here?"

"Yes, I want you to take everything off slowly. I want to see your body."

He was losing his patience as I just stood there frozen. Then, he continued in a sarcastic tone.

"Please, don't tell me you haven't done this before. I know you "American girls." Don't expect me to believe you are a virgin."

I dropped my head and looked down at the floor.

"Oh my God! You are a virgin. I truly am a lucky man," he chuckled. He proceeded in a loud voice, "Come on, and don't keep your husband waiting."

I was petrified when he got up and removed his pants because I had never seen a naked man before.

"We can do this the nice way or the hard way. You choose. Either you take your clothes off now or I will rip them off like an animal."

At that point, he really started to scare me. I knew he was capable of raping me although I already felt violated just by the way he looked at me. I reluctantly undressed for him, degrading myself once again.

He came close to me and pulled my hair down. I could smell the suffocating aroma of tobacco mixed with liquor on his breath. It was nauseating.

"Not bad," he said, as he looked me over. "Wash up. I want you nice and clean. I laid out what I want you to wear for our special night. Go, and don't take long. I'll be waiting."

I could tell he was aroused, especially now that he knew he was going to be my first. As I showered, I remembered all the stories I had heard from my college girlfriends about their first time. The body tingling in anticipation of that moment, the desire and excitement taking over their ability to think, the wonderful feeling of making love to someone they really cared about. None of those emotions were there for me.

As I slipped into a skimpy, revealing piece of clothing, I thought about how I had envisioned my first time and knew this was not the way it was supposed to be. I had saved myself for the perfect man, and now I was giving my body to a total stranger. I felt so disillusioned.

"What's taking so long?" he shouted snapping me back to reality.

"I'm coming."

When I stepped out, he slowly devoured me with his eyes and asked me to turn around.

"You look incredible. I want to see you like this every night. Come closer," he said pulling me towards him.

I was sickened as he pressed his naked body against me. He started kissing my neck, then took off my top, turned me around and started biting my breasts. I just wanted to vanish. I was tense, stiff as a board. I shut down as he ripped off my panties with his teeth. I was disgusted by his kisses and his touch. His body rubbing against mine made me cringe. I kept thinking how I was moments away from losing my dignity and myself to a ruthless, manipulative, egocentric man who would forever remind me how worthless I would always feel in his arms.

He grabbed me by the waist, threw me onto the bed, and climbed on top of me. He was hard and began to penetrate me ruthlessly and violently. As he thrust himself in and out of me, his moans grew louder and louder until he climaxed. My motionless body just laid there. Tears rolled down my face and my hands moved to wipe them quickly and to avoid giving him the pleasure of knowing that he had hurt me both physically and psychologically.

I was ashamed and in pain. I was revolted by his actions. Yet, I was well aware that this was just the beginning.

After he was done with me, Fouad checked his pristine white sheets for evidence to corroborate that I was truly a virgin. He found his proof. He was delighted. I was humiliated.

"Wasn't it amazing? Because, I have to tell you, you're probably the best I've ever had, and you being a virgin was such a sweet perk," he said.

"You make me sick," I replied.

"You'll get used to it. You have no choice," he said laughing. "I know of many women who would kill to be in your place. You should feel honored."

As I got up to walk away, he grabbed me tightly by the arm. "Where are you going?"

I frantically pulled my arm back and tried to set myself free. What was the worst he could do to me that he had not already done? I was crazed and spoke without thinking.

"To scrub my body and try to get your scent off my skin."

He shoved me back on the bed and pinned me down.

"You go when I tell you to go. This is my wedding night. From this day forward, you are mine and my smell will always permeate your body," he said looking down into my eyes.

"Don't provoke me again, Fatima. No woman talks to me like that and lives to tell about it." He bit my lip hard enough to draw a little blood. "Be careful my darling," he whispered wiping my lip with his tongue. "I wouldn't want to lose my temper."

As he rolled over and sat up, he reached for a cigarette on the nightstand and lit it. After taking a few puffs he stood up. "Let's take a shower and go to sleep," he demanded. "We have an early start tomorrow."

As I stepped into the shower, the water felt like needles hitting my skin. Not only did I hurt, but I noticed the bruises on my breasts, arms and thighs. I quickly washed myself off and as I turned to get out, Fouad stepped in.

"Where are you going, my dear?" he asked. "Did you think that we were done?"

All I could do was close my eyes as he began kissing me again and fumbling my breasts. I was ill and prayed that this time it would end quickly.

As I made my way back to the bed, it was difficult to walk. He had ripped me from the inside out. Each step was a painful reminder of his barbaric acts. I needed some sanity.

When he finally fell asleep, I slipped into my bathing suit and robe and headed downstairs to the pool. From that moment on, it would become my sanctuary.

As I submerged my swollen body in the water, hoping to cleanse my mind and soul from the repulsive experience I had just lived, I allowed my mind to drift to a time when my life was simpler; a time when my hopes and dreams promised me a bright future.

chapter 2

Sweet Sixteen

"Happy birthday, sleepy head," Jamila said as she crawled on my bed.

"What time is it?" I groaned in a groggy voice.

"Time to wake up."

"Seven thirty!" I said after looking at the clock before covering my face with the sheets. "Come back in about an hour."

"Ok," Jamila replied, disappointed as she walked towards the door.

Suddenly, I hopped out of bed.

"Gotcha! Come back here. I hardly slept last night with all the excitement," I said, giving her a big hug.

"I'm so nervous about tonight. All these important people..."

"Don't worry. Out of all the people coming, you are the most important one, my best friend," I said holding her hand.

Jamila's parents wanted her to have a better life than the one they could give her in Antarah, so they convinced her aunt Samira, our cook, to talk my father into allowing her to come live with us.

My father agreed to bring Jamila to Washington under one condition, that she would be treated like a daughter. I was thrilled with my parents' decision to make her a part of our family.

I loved Jamila. She was truly like a sister to me. We told each other everything. It was fun having her around especially on a day like today.

"So, did you decide on what to wear?" I asked her.

"Not yet, I need your help."

"Why don't we have Mahmoud take us shopping?"

"Great idea."

We giggled as we bounced on the bed. A knock at the door startled us.

"Keep it down, girls," Mama said, peering in.

"Come in, Mama."

"Happy sweet sixteen, habeebtee."

"Thank you," I said kissing both sides of her cheeks.

"Where's Baba? Is he still sleeping?"

"When have you known your father to sleep past 6 am?"

With that, I dashed out of the room and down the spiral staircase to his study.

The door was not fully shut, and I could hear him speaking Arabic, but could not make out the words. He was pacing. I detected anger in his voice and wondered if it had to do with tonight. He was an intimidating man especially when he was angry.

"What have I told you about listening behind my door?"

He was fuming.

"Sabah Al Khair, good morning, Baba," I said as he slammed the door in my face.

This was not the way I imagined starting out my day. Tears streamed down my face as I leaned back against the wall. It was my birthday and I had made my father angry.

I stood there for a couple of minutes when the door suddenly opened.

"Come in, Fatme, "he said in a sturdy voice. "I'm sorry, habeebtee. It has been one of those mornings and I shouldn't have taken it out on you. Eid Meelad Saeed, happy birthday!" he said wiping my tears. "I really don't know what got into me. Am I forgiven?"

"Of course, Baba."

"Are you sure?" he asked, giving me an apologetic kiss, dispelling my sadness.

"Yes," I said giving him a big hug. "I still can't believe we are having a party. You're the best, Baba."

"Don't thank me. This is entirely your mother's doing. You know I'm not that keen on these American customs."

"Oh, Baba! After all these years in this country…"

"Birthdays are not celebrated in Antarah. They're not celebrated in most of the Middle East, for that matter."

"Well, Alhamda Allah, thank God, we are in America," I said with a big smile and a kiss. "Baba, do you think Mahmoud can take Jamila and me to the mall?"

"It's up to your mother. I won't need him to drive me anywhere until this afternoon."

"Thank you, Baba. I'll let you work now."

"Tell Samira to bring me some coffee."

"Ok, Baba."

I was troubled. Something did not feel right. But it was my birthday. I did not want anything or anyone to ruin this day.

"Good morning khalti Samira."

Even though Samira wasn't my aunt, I refered to her as khalti because it implied respect for an older person that was like family. When my mother got married, my grandparents sent Samira to work for my parents because my mom could not fry an egg. My mother never denied the fact that she hated to cook. The only thing she enjoyed was making ahwa for my father and their guests. She was addicted to the coffee's flavor and the cardamom's aroma. That was probably why it had been the one thing she had mastered.

"Sabah Al Noor, good morning, habeebtee. Eid Meelad Saeed," Samira said hugging me and kissing me three times on each cheek. "Are you hungry?"she asked.

"Who can eat? I have butterflies in my stomach," Jamila replied.

"Me too," I said.

"Khalti, Baba wants ahwa."

"I'll make it," Jamila said.

"No, that's all right, I'll make it," Mama replied as she walked into the kitchen. "How's the cooking coming along for tonight, Samira?"

"Everything's on schedule, Mrs. Iman. All of Fatima's favorite dishes will be ready by this evening."

Samira spoiled us rotten. Every morning before we left for school, she would ask us what we wanted for dinner and then she would indulge us with our favorite foods. I loved to watch and help prepare traditional Arabic dishes. Unlike my mother, I enjoyed cooking. Stuffed grape leaves, lentil soup, hummus and babaghanoush were top on my list. Samira even prepared American delicacies. She was truly a fabulous cook.

"Samira, the caterers will arrive in the early afternoon, so make sure you leave them some room to work. Also, if you need them to help you arrange some of the food, just ask. Henri is aware that you are taking care of the Mediterranean dishes and he will assist you in any way he can. I want you to be out of this kitchen early so that you'll have enough time to dress for the party."

"Thank you, Mrs. Iman."

"We wouldn't have it any other way," I said giving her a big hug.

"You girls need to eat something. You have a long day ahead of you," Samira insisted.

"Khalti, we'll have plenty to eat tonight. Mama, can Mahmoud take Jamila and me shopping? We still need to get a few more things. I ran it by Baba and he left it up to you."

"Are you sure he doesn't need Mahmoud to take him somewhere?"

"Not until this afternoon."

"Okay, but just for a few hours. I want both of you rested for tonight."

A simple gathering with close friends and family would have been just fine, but there is no such thing as small and intimate when your father has a reputation for throwing some of D.C.'s most lavish parties. The ambassador and his wife were quite a team and had been for many years.

In 1970, my Baba, Gaffar Abdul Aziz, was instrumental in helping his close friend, Farris Saeed, overthrow the government of Antarah. When President Saeed took over, he rewarded my father by naming him head of the military police. Years later, he was appointed ambassador to the United States and relocated with my mother to the nation's capital.

Although my parents were eager to start a family, it wasn't till two years after they moved to the States that their prayers were answered.

For nearly six months, my mother was bedridden because of pregnancy risks. In the end, she gave birth to a 7 lbs. 9oz. girl. I was named Fatima after my father's mom.

I was the apple of my father's eye. I was his miracle baby. I was the fruit of their love. He was so proud to have a little girl. He nicknamed me Fatme. He also called me habeebtee, my love. That was my favorite.

My birthday was a special day to him because it was a reminder of the realization of his dream of fatherhood. Today was different. I could not forget the phone call that had rattled him and made me the victim of his wrath.

We lived in the exclusive neighborhood of Kalorama, which is Greek for "beautiful view". Kalorama sits on a hill above Dupont Circle and houses some of the greatest buildings in Washington D.C. It was a community filled with fancy mansions, elegant embassies, museums and some of D.C.'s most influential people. Tonight, many of those people would be attending my extravagant celebration.

As the evening approached, Mama helped us get ready. Jamila's mom, who was a seamstress in Antarah, had sent me a dress that she had designed and made especially for this day. It was a pale pink fitted, strapless, taffeta dress under a sheer, long sleeve lace dress. One sleeve fit like a glove and flared at the hand. The other was oversized and flowing like a bird's wing. Each peek of the diamond shaped lace pattern ended in a minute pink stone that made it sparkle. I wore my hair down and pulled back on each side with small pink flowers.

As I stood there looking into the mirror, Mama handed me a small, beautifully wrapped box.

"This is from your father. He wanted to be sure you had these for your 16th birthday."

As I quickly unwrapped my gift and opened it, I let out a gasp. My father had given me pink tourmaline earrings to match my dress.

"You look perfect!" Mama cried out after she applied a hint of strawberry gloss on my lips. "You have developed into quite a beautiful and sophisticated young woman. You both have," she said giving Jamila and me a hug.

Shortly afterwards, they rushed out of my room. It was almost 7 o'clock and they wanted to make sure that everything downstairs was just right.

Limos lined around the circular driveway as guests arrived. It was an evening of glamour. The women wore gowns by top designers and the men were equally fashionable in their penguin suits. The camera flashes blinded them as photographers rushed to capture every move of Washington's most elite. Walking into the foyer, they were captivated by the huge chandelier that hung from the center of the dome shaped ceiling. As they looked up, they admired the hand-painted sky mural surrounded by gold Arabic writing which read the 99 adjectives used to describe Allah.

"Gaffar, Iman, when did you have this done?" the Egyptian ambassador inquired.

"A few weeks ago. I actually had an Arabic writing specialist flown in to hand paint the lettering."

My father was proud of this room and made it the center of all our entertaining. Everyone always gathered around the beautiful, black baby grand to sing or just relax to the music. For this special evening, Baba had hired a pianist to play all the classic and popular American tunes.

As the pianist began playing "Daddy's Little Girl" I knew this was my cue to make my entrance. I stood at the top of the stairs and a hush fell over the room, Baba sung his version of Nat King Cole's "Unforgettable". My emotions took over, and with tears in my eyes, I made my way down through the crowd and into my father's arms.

"Thank you, Baba. That was beautiful."

"You are beautiful," he said gently wiping my tears.

This would be a night that I would never forget.

Finally, after hours of eating, drinking and dancing, I made a wish and blew out the sixteen candles on my cake.

The men assembled in my father's study. It was off limits as they gathered to drink ahwa and to smoke the argheele. I went into the hallway storage closet located behind Baba's library because, as a child, I often sneaked in there to play. One day I noticed a hole which allowed me to look into the study unnoticed. Many times I watched Baba as he worked in his study. Today, it was the perfect spot to peep and listen to what the men were saying.

"Gaffar, what kind of tobacco is this?"

"Who said anything about tobacco, it's the best hashish from the Middle East," he said while puffing on the bubble pipe.

Chuckling, they all looked at each other and wondered whether it was truly a joke.

Baba's study was surrounded by built-in bookshelves that housed mostly rare collections of Arabic books, including a signed first edition of "The Prophet" by Gibran Khalil Gibran and copies of the Holy Qur'an in every language that it had been translated.

There were also pictures of him with presidents, secretaries of state, and entertainers he had met throughout his political career.

Although Mama was usually careful not to disturb my father and his friends while they were in the study, on this night she knocked on the door to remind them that the belly dancer had arrived.

As the musicians started playing, the belly dancer made her way to the Arabian Nights-themed garden where men and women quickly gathered to watch the sensuous dance.

"I wish I could move like that," the wife of the Chinese prime minister said in a mischievous tone.

As I overheard the women, I smiled knowing that thanks to Mama, I had already mastered the fine art of belly dancing.

"It is the secret to a great waistline and a passionate marriage," Mama always said.

When my father was out of town, we would invite my girlfriends over for belly dancing lessons. We would crank up lively Arabic music, shake our hips and swerve our arms. That is the most fun I remember having with my mother, giggling and feeling that our whole lives were ahead of us.

Across the Atlantic

"Rauf tells me that you're from Antarah."

"That's right," she said as she twirled a ring on her right wedding finger with her thumb.

"I'm Major Fouad Mustafa," he said as he extended his hand to shake hers and held it a little longer than usual. "A pleasure meeting you."

"I'm Esmaa Al-Basheer," she responded unfazed by the long hand shake.

"So, Esmaa, what brings you to Shrivenham?" he asked pulling a chair out from a table for her to sit then taking a seat across from her.

"A semester abroad."

"A beautiful woman like you doesn't need an education, just a man to take care of her. Is that an engagement ring on your right hand?" he asked after signaling a waiter and ordering two espressos.

"No. It is to scare off unwanted Middle Eastern suitors, " she said in a sarcastic tone, "I neither need nor want a man to control my life. I left Antarah for exactly that reason."

"An overbearing father."

"And six brothers. I needed to breathe."

"You can't blame them for being over protective. It's the Arabic way."

"I was born in the wrong part of the world. I love the United States. After I graduate from Texas A&M, I want to work for NASA and go for my Masters."

"A Muslim, Arabic woman in NASA is quite a coup."

"Stirring up controversy is what I do best," she paused as she sipped her coffee. "I have to ask you. Are you Rauf's friend because he's the President's son?"

"Where did that come from?" he asked drinking his coffee as if it were a shot of liquor. "And so what if that were the case?"

"Rauf is a bore. I just can't imagine anyone being his friend for any other reason."

"One day, he will be the next president of Antarah."

"If someone doesn't kill him first."

"Smart and outspoken. I like that in a woman. What can I do to convince you to have dinner with me?" he asked as he held her hand.

"Just ask," she said slipping her hand from his and twirling her ring as she stared into his eyes.

"I like you, Esmaa Al-Basheer. You are a very intriguing woman; unlike any Antarahan woman I've met before."

"And I'm sure you've met many."

"Have I told you that you are also beautiful?"

"A couple of times. I'm sure you tell that to all the women you meet."

chapter 3

The Legend of Antarah

What a wonderful evening! It was like a fairy tale.I thought to myself. Samira and Jamila helped me carry the gifts to my room.

As I collapsed into my large canopy bed and stared at the hand painted flowers over the soft pink walls, I glared at my dresser and spotted a nicely wrapped box. At first, I thought it was a doll or a camel figurine to add to my collection. As I unwrapped it, I found a note that read: "For generations, this book has been passed down to the women in my family. Now, it's time for you to have it until you pass it on to the next generation of Antarahn women."

This was truly unexpected. I always wondered why my parents did not talk much about their upbringing or their lives in the old country. I often tried to ask Samira about my parents' lives in Antarah, but she always told me the same thing.

"I'm only an old cook."

My mother avoided my questions.

"That was a lifetime ago," she always replied.

Although I was tired, I started reading the book. For the rest of the evening, I read page after page and was unable to put it down. I was totally captivated by the story.

Soon, it was already morning and I heard a faint knock at the door. I looked up as Jamila slowly walked in.

"What are you reading?" she asked.

"A book on Antarah. It was a gift from Mama. I've been up all night. I couldn't put it down. Did you know that the name of the country is very symbolic? Listen to this." I read out loud: "Legend has it that Antarah was the knight of the desert, a warrior who won every battle, a hero among men. Antarah was also a poet, who was strong and sensitive.

He wrote his poems for his first cousin, the love of his life, Ablah," I paused and placed the open book on my lap. "Did you know that the Arab world encourages first cousin marriages as a way to protect family unity and wealth?"

"I know marriages between first cousins are very common in Antarah," Jamila replied.

"The book says that their love was so real yet so out of reach," I continued reading.

"How romantic!" Jamila sighed. "Tell me more."

"Despite Antarah and Ablah's many obstacles to fulfill their love, they did marry and live happily ever after. The poems he wrote for her were full of passion with an undying love that would transcend time and all its boundaries," I put the book against my chest as I allowed myself to dream.

"Jamila, I sense my parents had that same kind of passion for one another; the kind of love I hoped to find some day."

Mama walked in as we sat talking.

"You girls are already awake?"

"I haven't gone to sleep yet, Mama. I was up reading. Your gift was the best. Thank you," I said giving her a big hug.

"I'm so happy that you can appreciate it. It's such a romantic story. When I was your age, I dreamed of marrying someone like Antarah. I was blessed. Allah made that dream come true with your Baba."

"How did you two meet?"

"Why don't you get some rest and we can talk about it later."

"Come on, Mama."

"Please, Mrs. Iman," Jamila interjected.

"Ok. It was an arranged marriage," she said.

This was mind-boggling. I could not understand how she could marry someone she did not know or love.

"Love comes with time. He was my cousin, on my father's side, my aunt's first born. He was so handsome. When his family came to visit, I always made sure to look my best. I was worried he wouldn't like me because we never had an opportunity to talk. When no one was looking, we would glance into each other's eyes. I was hoping that he would give me some indication that he might be interested. Then, one day his father and the eldest men from the family came to talk to my father. They came to ask for my hand in marriage. After a dowry was decided, my father proudly accepted Gaffar's proposal to marry me. I was so happy I was going to be a wife. I was also anxious to be a mother," Mama said.

"But at least there was a spark between you."

"I guess there was."

"Marrying cousins, dowries, all that has really changed since those days, right?" I asked.

"Not back home," she said, "you are just so accustomed to this country you don't understand the way it is done in the Middle East."

I kept insisting about the love issue.

"How many people get married in this country based on love and wind up getting divorced a few years later?" she asked.

She had a point.

"Divorce rarely happens in our country. We stay together till death," she assured me.

"What about the four wives issue?" I asked.

"The Muslim religion allows a man to marry up to four wives as long as he can provide equal financial and emotional stability. When I thought I couldn't have a child, I encouraged your father to have a second wife. I wanted him to have children even if it meant sharing his love. He had the means but he chose not to do it."

"I totally disagree with the concept of multiple wives. Baba did the right thing. I would never accept my husband marrying another woman, under any circumstances."

"It's the man's decision," my mother insisted. "Don't start drilling your father about these issues. Let's keep this conversation to ourselves. You must be exhausted if you haven't gone to bed yet. Brush your teeth and get a few hours of sleep," Mama said giving us a kiss.

Jamila and I kept talking. She told me that she could not wait for her parents to call with the news that someone had asked for her hand in marriage.

"That's my dream. A nice Muslim man who can take care of me and with whom I can start a family," Jamila said.

"I want to pick my own husband. It has to be someone I am madly in love with," I replied.

"I'll be madly in love as time goes by. As long as he loves me, I will be happy," she insisted.

That was one topic Jamila and I could never agree on. Yet, I respected her ideas.

That was our first and last conversation about love and marriage. Jamila's shot at happily ever after had arrived sooner than I could have expected and within a few months she was on her way back to Antarah.

Jamila was beside herself. Everything had worked out as she hoped. She was getting her chance to meet prince charming. Her fiance was young, handsome and from a prominent family. He was actually a distant cousin. She was about to make her dreams of marriage and having a family of her own come true.

Although I was happy for Jamila, I was also devastated because I was losing my best friend. Her life was about to undergo a drastic change. She was about to become a wife.

Before she left, we vowed to write to each other, and we kept our promise. I missed her so much and was comforted to know that she was in love and happy. Marriage was everything she had imagined and more.

chapter 4

Love & Marriage

It had been months since I read the book on Antarah but I still had many unanswered questions. I felt so guilty breaking my promise to Mama but I had many restless nights trying to make sense of it all.

One morning, I made sure Mama was still asleep and rushed to Baba's study, locking the door. I needed a man's perspective, and who better to ask than the only man I trusted and respected.

"You're up early, habeebtee," he said.

"Baba, Mama gave me a book on Antarah for my birthday. She also made me promise not to burden you with questions about love, marriage…but I just need to know."

"What's this all about, Fatima?" he asked concerned.

"Before I ask you, please tell me that this will be our little secret. I don't want to disappoint Mama."

"Come here, habeebtee," he said lovingly. "You know that I'll always be here for you and will answer any question. This conversation will stay between us, I promise."

"Thank you, Baba," I said, kissing his hand.

"So, what do you want to know?"

"Why can a Muslim man marry up to four wives?"

"What does this have to do with the book on Antarah?"

"It just sparked a conversation one evening and that happened to come up."

"You know I'm not a religious man, but when I was a young boy I studied the Qur'an and asked many questions just like you. Islam gives a man permission to marry two, three, or four women only on the condition that he deals justly with them. He has to be fair with all his wives, and treat them equally, emotionally and financially, which is very difficult. For example, he has to provide separate living accommodations for each of his wives. Since it is very hard to be fair with all wives, in practice, most Muslim men do not do this. Therefore, having more than one wife in Islam is not a rule or an order, but an exception."

"But isn't this unfair to women?"

"The reason for multiple wives in Islam is not to satisfy men's desires, but for the welfare of the widows and the orphans of the wars. During war times, many women were unable to find husbands, so, many preferred to be a co-wife than to have no husband and father figure for their children."

"How about when Mama thought she couldn't have a baby?"

"If a man's wife is sterile and can't give him a child, he has the right to marry another woman. However, men are prohibited from cheating on their wives. A man can't marry another woman without his wife's consent because she might refuse such a request, and in this case it's her right to ask for a divorce. I had accepted Allah's will. I had no interest in any woman but your mother. I had come to terms with not being a father if that's what God wanted. Yet, your Mama loved me so much she was willing to share my love for me to become a father."

"She loves you so much, Baba."

"I love her too. So you see, women have rights in Islam. Don't think that men have all the power and can do whatever they want. A woman is a beautiful gift from Allah and she should get the utmost respect. I wouldn't want anything but the best for my habeebtee."

"Thanks, Baba," I said giving him a big hug. "I love you."

"I love you more sweetheart."

In England...

"I have a confession to make. Before I met you, I already knew about you. I read an article on you in some campus or town publication. I can't remember. I was driven to your ambition, determination, and passion. It reminded me of me."

"So Fouad, what exactly are you trying to tell me?"

"Isn't it obvious? I want you. I want to share my future with you."

"A future in Antarah. Are you out of your mind?"

"With Rauf's help, I'll move up the military ranks and become Antarah's next president."

"I have no doubt you'll go all the way. But president might be a stretch."

"Not with you by my side."

"What do you mean?"

"Wouldn't you like to be Antarah's first lady? Share the power and glory. Go to the United States and be recognized not only for your contributions to their country but also respected and praised for your efforts in Antarah."

"Of course."

"You'd have the world at your feet. All it would take is a plan. Sacrifices would have to be made, but in the end, we would have each other and everything we've ever wanted. I trust you and I need you."

Esmaa started unbuttoning Fouad's shirt and kissing his chest.

"I like the fact that you trust me," she whispered in his ear. "Talking to me about power is a real turn on."

"You are a real turn on," he said ripping her shirt off. "I usually take what I want, but I've waited patiently for this moment."

"I've wanted you since the day we met, but sometimes a girl needs to play hard to get."

"There's no room for games anymore."

"I know. I can't wait any longer. I want you now."

Fouad cleared a desk full of papers with a sweep of his arm and lifted her onto the hard, wooden surface. He started removing the rest of her clothing with fierce desperation. She responded in the same way. Undressed, he pinned her arms down with his strong hands and placed his entire fiery body over hers. He kissed her intensely leaving passion marks all over her delicate skin.

Then, when she begged him to satisfy her desires, their bodies came together until the moaning left them breathless.

Fouad slid off the table, lit a cigarette and sat on a chair.

"I'm glad you weren't my first," Esmaa said as she pulled herself up and stayed seated on the desk.

"Is that a compliment?"

"Yes," she said signaling for a drag of his cigarette. "If you would've been my first, you would've killed me. All that passion, who knew?"

"It was all bottled up inside just for you, Esmaa," he said getting up to continue where they left off.

"We need to talk," she said gently pushing his chest with her hand.

"I'm not going anywhere. What's wrong?"

"Were you serious earlier? About us? "

"Absolutely. I'm counting on your brains and your body to achieve my plans."

"Isn't that a little presumptuous of you?"

"Who are you kidding? We are one and the same. I knew it from the moment I laid eyes on you."

"How do you know I'm not working for Antarah's government and just using you to find out if you're a traitor?"

Wrapping his arm around her neck and pressing his body against hers, he softly whispered, "People who double cross me never live to talk about it."

"I would expect nothing less from you," she responded, as he loosened his grip allowing her to turn towards him.

As she began kissing his chest, she slid off the desk and worked her way down as she gave Fouad pleasure. He responded by carrying her to the bed and making love to her again and again.

After several hours, they showered. He put a robe on and she wore one of his shirts.

"Where do we go from here?" she asked removing a single cigarette from a pack.

"Business as usual," Fouad replied while lighting her cigarette. "You go back to Texas and finish your nuclear engineering degree. I go back to Antarah and play the role of Rauf's devoted friend, get close to the president and earn my promotions. We see each other sporadically until I get closer to our target."

"And, how much time are we looking at?"

"A few years, maybe longer. As long as it takes to succeed. Can you wait that long?"

"Do I have a choice?"

"No."

"Well Fouad, what I want are four to five years to achieve my personal goals," she said putting out her cigarette then twirling her ring with her thumb.

"What you want is irrelevant if I need you before then." He put out his cigarette.

"I'll be ready. Just let me know."

"Enough talk. Come here," he proceeded tearing off her shirt. "I leave for Antarah tomorrow so, let's make tonight unforgettable."

chapter 5

A Loss

few years had passed since my sweet sixteen. Now, I was starting a new chapter in my life. After graduation, I enrolled at Smith College in Massachusetts to major in psychology. I picked Smith not only for it's fine reputation among women's colleges but also, because it offered a Master's in Social Work, which was my career goal.

I was a grounded young woman, eager to help others. During my travels, I had seen a lot of poverty and suffering. I wanted to make a difference in the world and thought this would be a beginning.

I loved college life. I was out of the house, was more independent, did not have my usual watchdogs and made my own decisions. I had many friends, a few brief romances, nothing like Antarah and Ablah, and a lot of temptations.

Yet, I always remembered my father's words, "All you have is your honor and the honor of your family name."

I was in my third semester of college when I came home for four days to celebrate the Muslim holiday, Eid. It was a joyous time. All of our family who lived in the States gathered at our house for this celebration. Samira prepared our favorite dishes and sweets. The house was filled with love and laughter.

This year was different. Everyone was there but all the laughter had turned to sadness. My mother had been diagnosed with cancer three months earlier. I was kept in the dark until I arrived home.

My mother, who was bedridden, asked to see me right before her passing.

"Habeebtee Fatme, you're the biggest gift Allah has ever given me. When I found out I was pregnant, I thought I would burst with excitement. You've been an ideal daughter. You've made me proud and have filled my life with a happiness I never knew existed. I was blessed with your love and your father's love. My life was better than I could have ever imagined. My sickness is Allah's will. Don't cry for me. Instead, thank God for the life we had together and for all of God's blessings."

Tears just rolled down my cheeks. I felt it was so unfair that she would not be by my side on my graduation day, my wedding day, and my child's first birthday.

She wiped my tears and took off her favorite bracelet with a heart locket.

"This is for you. Your father gave it to me when we got engaged. I want you to keep it so you can always remember me and all the happiness we shared," Mama said. "You and your father are my heart."

I immediately put it on my wrist and opened the heart. There was a tiny picture of my father and me. Three days later, she passed away.

The bracelet was the only piece of jewelry I never took off. This always made me feel like I had a piece of her with me.

Shocked and in disbelief, I was angry with my father for keeping her illness from me. Had I known, I would have spent those last months by her side.

"Habeebtee, I'm so sorry but your mother didn't want to disturb your studies," he said "I went along with her wishes. If it makes you feel better, I spent a lot of time with her and did my best to make her happy."

I could see he was holding back his tears. After thirty-two years of marriage, I really did not know how he would go on without her. I hugged him and reassured him that everything would be all right. He pulled himself together for my sake, although I knew inside he was devastated. The day she died was the saddest day of our lives.

It was such a relief to be surrounded by family. In the Muslim religion, the closest family members of the deceased have to cleanse the body (males if the deceased is a man, females for a woman). My two aunts and I washed my mother's body and then wrapped it in a white cloth before placing it in a wooden box to be transported to Antarah.

My father and one of my uncles would accompany my mother's remains to bury them by my grandparents' side. According to our beliefs, the body had to be buried within 24 hours of the person's passing. Therefore, I did not have much time to mourn by my father's side. I had to stay on his behalf with the rest of the family to receive all the people that would be coming to pay their respects.

Right before my father left for the airport, the President of the United States and the President of Antarah called offering their condolences. My mother was very loved and respected, especially in the political circuit, because she was involved in many philanthropic organizations.

Dignitaries and friends gathered at our house offering their sympathy and support. Our sheik, Muslim cleric, was at the house reading from the Qur'an and praying for Allah to bless my mother's soul.

Samira must have served at least a thousand cups of ahwa, my mom's favorite beverage. It is customary after you've eaten or had coffee to say "daeeme" to forever be blessed with more of the same. But, when people die, you substitute "daeeme" with "Rahmatu Allah Alleijem," God's mercy on her/his soul.

It was a very difficult time for me, especially with my father and Jamila, my two closest loved ones, in Antarah. I guess I had never prepared for life without Mama.

When my father left to go to Antarah, Jamila had reassured me that she would be there to comfort him through this difficult time. She and her husband had already made all the arrangements to bury my mother quickly. A few of my mother's relatives who still lived in Antarah, including her oldest brother, would also be there.

Samira felt it was important for me to know the ritual that took place when a Muslim person died. She believed it was time for me to learn more about my religion and she knew that, with Mama gone, she was the closest I had to a mother figure.

"Before the body arrives" she told me, "a grave is dug perpendicular to the Qiblah, the direction in which a Muslim should pray, and the body is placed in the grave on the right side facing the Qiblah. According to Islam, the husband is not supposed to touch his wife after her death. So, another male family member, a son, father or brother, is assigned to lower the body. The wrapped body is taken out of the wooden box and placed on the ground with a piece of wood or stones to protect it so dirt does not fall directly on the body. A sheik reads passages from the Qur'an and asks for Allah to bless their soul. Afterward, the opening is covered with dirt."

My father told me he placed three white roses on Mama's grave, one from him, one from me and one from Jamila who she loved like a daughter.

I never knew how much I would miss her and need her considering the change my life was about to undergo.

chapter 6

Life Turned Upside Down

It had been a year since my mother's passing when my father received a very disturbing call. I was home for spring break, which coincided with Eid. My father was in his study. I could hear his loud voice in Arabic trembling with anger and a thumping sound as he paced on the hardwood floor. I put my ear against the door to try to listen. Suddenly, he paused and pounded on his desk. It startled me and I remembered the morning of my sixteenth birthday. I couldn't understand what was being said, but this behavior was very unusual for the general who kept his composure at all times. My gut told me he was speaking to the same person from years ago.

I had never heard my father sob, not even when my mother died, until that evening. I wondered what was wrong.

My mother had always been protective of my father's private space and always warned me about asking too many questions. A powerful man like him probably had his share of enemies. I started to wonder, did he have secrets he might be hiding, and if so were they coming back to haunt him?

The next morning, Baba called me into his study. He was nervously flicking the beads of the masbaja. Then, in a very official manner, as if he were giving a military order and referring to me by my full name, he spoke.

"Fatima, right after graduation, we will be going to Antarah to meet Lieutenant Fouad Mustafa, who has requested my permission to marry you. I have accepted his request. He is the only son of one of my closest and dearest childhood friends. He comes from a respectable family. He has a solid military background with a bright future ahead of him. You will marry Lt. Mustafa and live with him in the homeland. After the religious ceremony, I will return here to my diplomatic duties. He's given me his word that he will take good care of you. He has agreed on a new furnished home and approximately ten thousand dollars in gold jewelry. You will live very comfortably, the way you have been accustomed to. I think you've done very well for yourself."

In that instance, my whole world crumbled. I felt as if my life had been sucked right out of me. All the prehistoric notions and cultural conceptions I had criticized and denounced were becoming part of my reality. I snapped out of it.

"Are you out of your mind?" I said outraged. "You expect me to leave my friends, my home, and my life to chase after this stranger in Antarah. That's ludicrous and I just won't do it."

"Fatima, you have no choice."

"What do you mean? I'm a grown woman. If Mama were alive, she would never allow this."

"Your mother knew that this day would come and agreed that this was a wise decision. Are you going to go against her wishes?"

"I can't believe you're using Mama's memory to blackmail me into this"

I kept hearing Mama's voice, "Don't question your father? Just do as he says." I felt that this was what she was trying to tell me all along. But, what was I going to do in a land that I had never been exposed to? I had no family there and no mother to give me advice and tell me that it was going to be all right. My only comfort was reuniting with Jamila.

I was going to marry a man I didn't know and didn't love. This was infuriating and scary. I was frightened of the future and even more afraid of disappointing Mama. I knew my parents had my best interest at heart. I also knew the general wouldn't go back on his decision. Defying his authority would go against everything they taught me. I wiped the tears from my face.

"I'll do this for Mama's memory but I'll never forget the day you sold me to a perfect stranger like a whore."

He raised his hand at me but couldn't go through with it.

"I'm so disappointed and angry at you. I can't stand being here a minute longer." I walked away, defeated, then turned to face him. "Don't try to call me unless you come to your senses and change your mind. I'll see you in May."

It was the first time leaving my house without kissing Baba good-bye.

I returned to Smith and wrote to Jamila explaining my unexpected twist of fate. I also waited for my father to call and tell me it had all been a joke, a big mistake, but the phone call never came.

A week later, Samira called to tell me that my father had suffered a minor stroke the day I left. He had honored my wishes of not calling me unless he had a change of heart. I immediately went home and spent the weekend by his side but never discussed our last conversation.

Back in college, I started to write him a letter explaining that I was leaving; I was disappearing because I couldn't go through with his plans. I just couldn't do it. I couldn't betray the two people I loved most in this world; Mama who had shaped me into who I was and Baba who had taught me about family honor. Most importantly and probably the only reason I gave in to the general's request: I had already lost Mama and I couldn't bear the idea of being responsible for losing Baba.

The man who I knew deep in my heart had almost ruined my sixteenth birthday was also about to ruin my entire life. I was doomed to a loveless marriage in a country and a culture that I really didn't know. My fate had been sealed with one simple phone call and I had to leave it in Allah's hands.

chapter 7

The Meeting

I arrived in Antarah with Baba sporting a black, pin-striped dress suit revealing a little cleavage and some leg, and black, high- heeled pumps. It was important to wear something that made me feel in control and professional. After all, I was about to make the biggest business transaction of my life.

At the airport, we were given the red carpet treatment. Our passports were stamped; we didn't have to go through customs and no suitcases were opened. I was relieved because of a very meticulously packed trunk filled with nearly one hundred camel figurines.

When I was a child, I remember Baba taking me to the zoo. I was so overwhelmed looking at all the animals. When we got to the camel exhibit, I asked him, "Why do camels have humps?"

"The humps are fatty tissue. If the camel can't find food, it uses the fat for energy. Camels are called "the ships of the desert" because thousands of years ago, in southern Arabia, camels were used as transportation for people and goods that were imported and exported throughout the different countries".

"Is it true that camels can go days without water?"

"Yes. Camels were the perfect animals for long, hot trips because they can go without drinking for up to 7 days then drink 21 gallons of water in 10 minutes," he explained.

"Do camels live for a long time?"

"Camels can live for 40 years. They also have great memories. An abused camel will not act immediately, but will wait for years then turn on its abuser. "

After learning all those facts, I told him that the camel was my favorite animal.

"It is smart, useful, unique and has the most beautiful eyes," I told him.

From that day on, every trip Baba took, whether abroad or in the United States, he would always stop at a specialty shop to buy me a stuffed camel or statuette. He told me it had become a challenge to find camels since they weren't very popular animals. These camels represented my very special childhood, a time when life was magical and I cherished every moment with Baba.

At the airport, we were greeted by military personnel, mostly close friends of my father's. He always made it a point to bring them American cigars.

An official car awaited us. I was surprised, though, that my husband-to-be wasn't among the welcoming party.

As we rode in the car, I noticed pictures and paintings of the president plastered everywhere. It was as if the entire country was a shrine to him. I had come across this trend in many of my travels through the Middle East. It was actually quite common for establishments and homes to display pictures of the president. This meant that you were a political supporter. If you chose not to exhibit his image, it might be interpreted as not being fully supportive of the government, maybe even being a traitor.

I never understood how the people of these predominantly Muslim countries allowed their president to assume this "mightier than God" role. I imagined it was out of fear. But, what was really disturbing was how a devout Muslim president would allow his people to worship him as if he were God. This was the kind of thought process that could really get me in trouble.

Now that we were here, the first thing I wanted to do was visit my mother's grave. I missed her so much. I needed to be close to her and tell her how my life was in turmoil.

"Fatme, you know women aren't allowed to visit the cemetery. We'll stop and pick up some white roses and I'll put them on her grave."

Baba explained that over the grave stood a cinder block structure about three feet high, three feet wide and six feet long, painted in white. On top of the structure were two pieces of marble on each side; one representing the head, facing the East towards Mecca, and the other the feet. Between the marble pieces and centered on the blocks was a marble tombstone with the word Fatiha, prayer from the Qur'an, and under it her name, her date of birth and date of death in Muslim calendar years.

While Baba went to place the flowers on Mama's grave, I stayed with the driver on the street. For a few minutes, I stepped out of the car for some fresh air. It was the closest I could be to my mother, and I felt her presence.

"Mama, you left when I need you the most. I miss you so much. I need your advice. I need you to hold me and assure me that everything is going to be all right. I'm afraid. My life is headed in an unexpected direction and I don't know if I'm doing the right thing. I didn't question my father's judgment because you always told me not to defy his authority. If you were here, I know you would have spoken to Baba and convinced him that this marriage isn't right. I guess there is nothing that can be done now," I told myself.

Baba returned shortly after. I could tell that he was sad. He had truly aged since my mother's passing. I think his dedication to his work was the only thing keeping him alive.

The car took us straight to the Presidential Palace. I was somewhat nervous. I had met President Saeed twice when he visited Washington but I was just a child then.

The palace was beautiful and very different from the White House. It was isolated from any neighborhood and in the outskirts of the capital. Two square miles of the palace were heavily secured. The exterior of the structure was an off white marble. The interior architectural design was very impressive with huge columns, marble floors and majestic hand carved ceilings. The walls were white with a pearl finish and were mostly decorated with countless portraits of the president ranging in size and painted by different artists from around the world. There were also huge plaques with passages from the Qur'an.

Enormous Persian rugs with rich colors and flowery designs covered large flooring areas. The dinning room could seat at least fifty guests for a formal dinner. Adorning the formal living room were more than 75 chandeliers hanging from a 16- foot ceiling. All the furniture was custom made and covered by exotic fabrics.

Many rooms had cultural artifacts such as instruments from the region. There was a collection of beautiful, hand carved and painted wooden boxes which could be used to play shutrange, chess and dama, backgammon. Also, a large glass casing that displayed objects of ancient Roman times.

Two enormous doors opened into an informal meeting room. The first thing that caught my eye was a beautiful portrait of the president with his wife, three daughters, and a son.

As I looked around, I saw several men dressed in uniform and a few women, among them the president's wife and his youngest daughter, Rania. She was the only one of the three daughters that still lived at home. Rania was 18, with shoulder length dark hair and the least attractive of the three.

As I watched the men greet each other with a customary kiss on each cheek, I tried to guess which one of them was the one I would be marrying. I just bowed with my head acknowledging them but not looking them in the eye. The women immediately approached me and kissed me on each cheek.

"Mabruk, congratulations," they said referring to my upcoming nuptials.

Rania stood silently in the back and only greeted me with a smile. I immediately sensed a certain tension without really knowing why.

Suddenly, President Saeed made his entrance.

"Assalamu Alaykum, peace be with you," he said.

"Wa Alaykum Assalam, peace be with you," everyone responded as a group.

The president walked up to us, hugged and kissed my father and then hugged me.

"Welcome to Antarah," he told me.

"Thank you, Mr. President."

"You have turned into a beautiful young woman," the president said. "The last time I saw you, you were just a child. I hear congratulations are in order. You are marrying one of Antarah's most eligible bachelors, one of my proteges and my son Rauf's best friend."

Rania, who now stood by her father, seemed saddened by his comment. I thanked the president and out of the corner of my eyes, I saw two men in their early to mid thirties enter the room.

"Here they are now. My son, Colonel Rauf Saeed and Lieutenant Fouad Mustafa. This is Fatima Abdul Aziz," he said.

First impressions are lasting. Unfortunately, I was not too impressed. Fouad was a light skinned, six-foot tall man. He had typical Arabic features: a large nose, brown eyes, and short, wavy, dark hair with a touch of gray. The slight gap between his two front teeth made his grin appear fake. He was not bad looking, but he was not my type. There was something about him that made me uneasy. Maybe it was the way he carried himself, like he was God's gift to women. I do not know why, I just felt I could not trust him.

The moment was awkward. I did not know if I should speak or extend my hand. All I could do was look down and wait for him to make a move. He spoke in broken English.

"Welcome to Antarah," he said as I looked up and smiled although my first instinct was to run and keep running until I could disappear.

I just did not have the guts to do it. I stood there patiently while I felt him discretely looking at me. This made me very uncomfortable. It was as if he was examining his prize to see if it measured up to his expectations.

Lieutenant Mustafa took my father to the side. I suspected they were making some kind of arrangement. After what seemed like a lifetime, my father came back and told me he had instructed the driver to take me to visit Jamila.

"But father, what about you?" I said.

"Fatme, unfortunately, I can't go. It is customary for the father of the bride to spend some time with his future son-in-law before the wedding. Please, tell Jamila I will see her within the next few days."

I used this opportunity to escape my fate just a little longer.

It was a beautiful afternoon. Antarah was exactly as I imagined it. I remembered the book Mama gave me on my sixteenth birthday that described the streets, the people, the beauty of the Old World, the houses made of stone and the cars stopping to let a herd of sheep cross the highway. It was so different from my life in the States and yet so refreshing.

As we entered the city, I could smell the ocean and I felt the breeze caressing my face. We were entering a modern looking neighborhood with tall buildings, many of them close to completion. They all looked pretty uniform, with marble facades and fancy entrances. I felt Jamila had done well for herself, and walked up the stairs to the fourth floor because the elevator was still under construction.

I knocked at the door and couldn't wait to see the expression on Jamila's face. She had no details of my arrival to Antarah because I wanted to surprise her.

I couldn't wait to hug her and talk to her about our lives. I also hoped she had some insight on Fouad because her husband, Nabil, was also a military man.

Our reunion was better than expected. Jamila was thrilled to see me and I was ecstatic to see that she was a few months pregnant. Although she was glowing as most expectant mothers do, I could sense that she was a little upset because of my unannounced visit. Jamila hated surprises as a child and it was apparent that time had not changed that.

"I didn't write to tell you about the baby because I wanted to surprise you for a change," Jamila said with tears in her eyes and a disappointed look on her face. "Why didn't you let me know that you were coming? I would have met you at the airport and prepared all your favorite dishes. Where's amee?"

I explained that Baba was tired because of the long journey but that he promised to come spend time with her within the next couple of days.

Jamila's apartment was very luxurious. It had exquisite Persian rugs over marble floors and custom-made furniture with rich, velvety materials framed in highly detailed, carved wood. Her balcony had a spectacular view of the ocean.

"You have a beautiful home, mabruk!" I said.

It was already late afternoon. Nabil was still at work, so Jamila and I walked across the street to the corneesh, the boardwalk along side the ocean.

The Mediterranean sunset was breathtaking. All my troubles just seemed to vanish with the wind and swept away with the waves if only for that instant and as the sun, I was ready to fade into an uncertain abyss without knowing if I would arise the next morning.

As we spoke of my impending marriage, Jamila looked into my eyes and saw my sadness.

"Fatima, maktub. Just accept your fate. You can't change your destiny. If you believe in Allah, you will embrace your future with Fouad and be happy."

"Jamila, you know that I never believed in arranged marriages. I never even thought I would step foot in Antarah. My parents never brought me here, they hardly spoke about this country and they never, ever prepared me for the possibility of an arranged marriage. You knew as a child that an arranged marriage was your fate. You accepted it and even looked forward to it, not me. My dreams and hopes were in America. I wanted to get my Master's in Social Work, help the less fortunate and use my political connections to make a difference."

"The people of Antarah need you more than the Americans and what more political connection than the president?"

"You have a point but how can I truly be happy here without my father, my friends… I thank Allah for you because no one else can help me through this. Have you asked Nabil if he knows anything about Fouad?"

"Besides the obvious, that he is well connected and best friends with the president's son, Nabil tells me Lieutenant Mustafa is well respected and feared. Off the record, many say he is ruthless and will do anything to get what he wants. But that could be a good quality. You need a strong man to challenge you and balance your rebellious side. You should be honored by his interest in you; he is after all one of the most sought after bachelors in the entire Middle East."

"You know things like that don't impress me. 'Ruthless' and 'feared' aren't very flattering attributes for a husband-to-be. I just can't imagine what I'm getting myself into."

"Fatima, please, don't discuss any of this with Nabil when you see him. I don't want to put him in an awkward position."

When we returned to Jamila's house, I met Nabil. He was a soft spoken, warm and friendly man. He looked at Jamila like only a man in love would look at a woman. He went in the kitchen with her and helped bring the food to the table. He then asked Jamila to sit with me while he got the bread. When we were eating, he insisted that Jamila eat more because she was eating for two. You could tell that he was very excited with the idea of being a father. He also kept asking me if I wanted more water, if I needed more bread; he was very attentive. I was truly delighted for my best friend. She had found a man that worshiped her.

After a lovely dinner, I returned to the Presidential Palace. When I arrived, it seemed that everyone had already gone to bed. On my way to my bedroom, Rauf, the president's son, startled me.

"Good evening, Fatima. My friend Fouad is truly a very fortunate man."

I just said good night and went into the room. I felt Rauf was flirting with me and I wasn't bothered by it. At this point, anyone seemed nicer than Fouad.

The next morning, while my father and the President discussed politics over coffee in the study, I had a cup of zoorat, a tea made from a variety of flowers in the garden. Minutes later, I was joined by Rauf.

"I thought it wasn't proper for us to be alone," I said.

"You are telling me this coming from America," Rauf replied.

"Living in America didn't make me forget the Arabic customs."

As I told him this, I looked into his deep blue eyes and noticed a very handsome man.

He wasn't as tall as Fouad but he had a mustache that made him look very distinguished and he was as charming as his father.

"Does my presence offend you?"

"No, but it might offend our parents," I said in a sarcastic tone.

"My mother left early and our fathers won't be around for a while. Is there anything you'd like to ask me?"

"If you mean about Fouad, I don't think anything you say is going to change the fact that I will be marrying him soon."

"Do I detect hostility in your voice?"

"Do I detect you're fishing for information to run and tell your friend?

"A true gentleman wouldn't betray a woman's confidence."

"Well, I hardly consider you my confidant. I'll just say that the idea of an arranged marriage does not sit well with me. I find the idea ludicrous. But, quoting the words of my best friend Jamila: "it is maktub" so I just have to accept it and hope for the best.

"Fatima, in Fouad's defense, he is a great man. Up till recently he was considered one of the Middle…"

"…East's most eligible bachelors. I know, I can't tell you the number of times I've heard that. So, why hasn't a thirty five-year-old catch like him been snatched?" I questioned.

"He is very focused. He wanted to be established in his military career. He wanted to have more time to devote to a family and I guess he feels he's reached that point."

Before he could go on about Fouad I interrupted. Unfortunately, nothing he could say would change my mind.

"It was nice talking to you but I have to run. I have a wedding to plan."

"Let me know if I can be of assistance to you, Fatme."

"The name is Fatima and no thanks, Colonel Saeed. I don't think there is anything anyone can do for me."

I was taken aback when he refered to me as Fatme. Only my father called me Fatme, an endearing nickname for Fatima used in the Middle East. I didn't feel comfortable with anyone else calling me this, especially a stranger. The only other person who I would accept calling me Fatme would be a man I truly loved, and unfortunately, I didn't think I would hear that from anyone else's lips but Baba's.

I went to my room and started one of what would become my traditional crying sessions. Half an hour later my father knocked at the door.

"Are you ready to go see Jamila?" he asked.

"Yes, Baba."

When we arrived at Jamila's, she had a table filled with our favorite dishes.

"Habeebtee Jamila, mabruk for the baby. I feel as proud as a grandfather would," Baba said.

"Amee, Ahlanwasahlan, welcome to my humble home," Jamila said.

"Why did you go through all this trouble, especially in your condition?" Baba asked.

"This is your first time in my house, amee. I needed to do something special for my favorite uncle."

Nabil joined us moments later. After lunch, he and my father drank ahwa and smoked the arguile in the balcony, while Jamila and I cleaned up and chatted about our days in D.C.

"Do you miss Washington?" I asked.

"I missed you, but now that you are here, my life is complete," Jamila replied.

I gave her a big hug and told her I was happy to be reunited with her.

Our visit was cut short by a phone call from Fouad. He wanted my father and me to meet him at the courthouse to sign a prenuptial agreement.

That was one thing my father had insisted on to protect my rights before entering this marriage. This agreement was to include polygamy issues and financial responsibilities in case of divorce.

When we arrived to the courthouse, Fouad was waiting with the engagement rings. "I thought we would skip the engagement party and just have a lavish wedding. I know your father doesn't have much time in Antarah so this will speed up the process," he said.

Fouad opened a red velvet box that had two matching bands. In Islam, gold is permitted for women because they are delicate and gentle in nature, but not for men because it is seen as a sign of instability, weakness, and is un-masculine. Therefore, Fouad's wedding band was platinum, while mine was white gold.

He proceeded to place the smaller band around my finger on the right hand, and he handed me the other to place on his finger. In the Middle East, wearing the band on the right hand symbolizes that the person is engaged.

Minutes later the judge appeared. He was an old friend of my father's who had visited us in Washington several times. My father and Fouad greeted him with the traditional kiss on each cheek. I nodded politely acknowledging his presence.

"You look even more beautiful, if that's possible, than when I saw you on your sixteenth birthday party. Fouad is a lucky man," he said.

I smiled although deep inside I wanted to cry. I was handing over my youth and my being with someone that I knew I could never love. I was minutes from signing my life away.

The judge began to write in a record book that Fouad was to provide me with a new furnished house as part of our marriage contract. If I divorced him, I wouldn't be entitled to anything, but if he divorced me, I would get to keep not only the house, but one hundred thousand dollars. I agreed to these terms.

When the issue of polygamy came up, I refused that possibility. I knew Fouad was testing the waters to see how far he could go. I did not love him but I wasn't going to play second fiddle to another or several other women. On a personal level, I considered it an insult and consequently, an added complication that I was not willing to gamble with.

I clearly stated that if he were to marry another woman it would be solid grounds for divorce and, under those circumstances, I would retain all my financial rights.

I realized Fouad was pleased with the passion I displayed concerning other wives. He definitely had mistaken my outrage with the possibility of me developing feelings for him. Certainly, that was not the case.

After everything was agreed upon, we signed on the dotted line.

In my mind, money was never an issue. I knew I was the sole heir to all my father's assets including our Washington estate. Most importantly, I had an education, a career and contacts I could rely on if necessary.

Nevertheless, I wondered if Fouad knew the extent of my father's wealth and if that was an added incentive for this union.

Financially, he was well-off but I knew that a few more American dollars couldn't hurt.

I didn't dwell on the financial aspect because I trusted that my father was wise enough to know what he was getting me into.

After the judge indicated that all the documents were complete, Fouad took my hand and kissed it. I felt his intense desire for me, and I was totally repulsed by that prospect.

The next morning, we had a small gathering at the Presidential Palace with President Saeed's family, Jamila and her husband, Fouad's sisters, their husbands and my father. The sheik was there to perform the religious ceremony.

Minutes before we said the "I do's", Rauf discretely whispered in my ear.

"If I would have known you first, I would have snatched you for myself."

"I thought you guys were best friends," I told him.

"We are, but you can't blame a man for admiring a beautiful woman."

I can't deny there was an attraction between us, but the reality was that I couldn't embrace the idea of being the future first lady of Antarah.

The sheik began by reading some passages from the Qur'an related to marriage. Then, we swore to love and to cherish each other in front of God and our witnesses. We were officially husband and wife. The marriage was not to be consummated nor the rings exchanged until after the wedding celebration, one week later.

At this point, Fouad and I would be able to go out alone, hold hands and kiss. I was buying time, avoiding as much contact with him as possible. Luckily, Nabil left on military assignment and would not be back until one day before the wedding. So, I took Jamila everywhere.

Jamila was so excited for me especially when we went to pick out the gold. As I was never really a big fan of jewelry, this was not a thrilling event. I felt uncomfortable with the idea of this man buying me things. I knew I would have to eventually pay him back somehow. Jamila assured me that gold was a symbol of love and status. The more gold, the more the man loved you. What's love got to do with it? He didn't know me. He was just adorning me like a Christmas tree. More than anything else, this was a stroke to his ego; a way to announce to all the women who were interested in him that they had missed out on a great catch and he was now officially off the market.

A man like Fouad could not be a saint. I could sense he was very experienced and had probably made many promises and broken many hearts. "After all, he was one of the most eligible bachelors…" I told myself sarcastically.

Jamila kept pulling me to the side and urging me to smile and act a little more excited. She felt I was provoking him to make a scene because I showed no appreciation as he showered me with gifts.

Fouad insisted in placing one of two choker necklaces around my neck. My hair was long, thick and curly. As he lifted it, he asked Jamila to hold it up until he put it on me. After he secured it, Jamila let my hair down and moved to the side to admire it. Fouad gently and discretely kissed my neck. I felt chills up my spine. Then, he told the storeowner to pack ten solid gold bangle bracelets and 4 rings.

"Do you like it? It is even more beautiful on you."

"Thanks but I'm not used to all this gold and I feel very uncomfortable," I replied.

"I want to buy this for you and I want to see all of it on you," he said almost whispering. "I want my woman to show off her husband's gifts. I forgive your ignorance because I know you are coming from America where you can say and do as you please."

As he pressed his body tightly close to mine and slightly pulled my hair he continued.

"You are in Antarah now and you do as your husband says. I also know you have been avoiding me. From now on, I want you to respond to my gestures of affection. I am not playing games and I will not be embarrassed by you."

I should have known something like this would happen, after all Jamila warned me.

Fouad had each piece of jewelry placed in beautiful decorative boxes and would formally give them to me during the wedding celebration. Fouad told Jamila to take me shopping for clothes for our honeymoon. Jamila insisted on going to a lingerie shop to get something special for my wedding night. I was very anxious about this but I knew I had to be prepared. My personal hell was about to begin.

"Is Fouad going to let you go out of the house without wearing the hijab?" Jamila asked with curiosity.

"I don't see why not. He hasn't brought anything up about me covering my hair and he knows that I have never done it before. Why do you ask?"

"Many men get very protective after they get married. Fouad seems like the jealous type and he probably feels you are too liberal and will want to clip your wings a little."

"I just won't allow it."

"Fatima, don't start your marriage on the wrong foot. Just go with it. Try to see the positive in him. Start falling in love with him. If you don't put some effort into it you will regret your life."

"Regret what life? With this man, I have no life. I'm desperate. I want to die. You wanted this life. I had no choice. Do you feel any compassion? First, I lose my mother and now this. I thought you were my sister. Did you even try to talk some sense into my father?"

I broke down in tears while Jamila tried to console me.

"What are we even doing here? Do you really think I can do this? I'm terrified. I've never been with a man in my life."

I was in a frenzy.

"Calm down, Fatima. You know there is nothing I can do but give you sound advice based on my life in Antarah. I can't confront your father about your marriage. I am not family. I'm so sorry I haven't been sensitive to your feelings; I just hoped that some part of you wanted this too. I was so happy to have you back in my life I didn't think…"

"I'm sorry, Jamila. You are just trying to make this a little easier. I just can't accept that this is my life now. I'm not even attracted to him. I prayed for there to be some kind of spark between us, but all I feel is contempt, hatred."

Jamila gave me a big, heart-felt hug.

"I can't change your fate but I'll be here for you whenever you need me. That's a promise I can keep."

In some way, Jamila's words gave me comfort.

The week passed too quickly. Fouad, Rauf and my father had taken care of all the last minute arrangements. My husband-to-be and his best friend had actually been planning this day for months.

Fouad was obsessed with the idea that all the "who's who" of Antarah would be there. Security was going to be extremely tight. After all, the president would be in attendance together with the most powerful people in the country and some other guests from the Middle East. It was a major production.

The wedding celebration was held at the Sahara, the fanciest restaurant/reception hall in Antarah. The place was swarming with secret service. There were over three hundred guests, mostly acquaintances of the groom.

When I walked in with my father, the whole room had their eyes on me. I wore a beautiful white silk, strapless, fitted dress with rhinestone buttons in the back and a silk wrap covering my shoulders. My hair was pulled back and over it laid a very simple veil with a rhinestone tiara.

The guests had filled the room with flower arrangements, a traditional gesture to congratulate the newlyweds. In one of the corners of the room, there were five circular tables, each one carrying a four-tier wedding cake lavishly decorated with fresh, red roses. In the middle of the room was an elaborately decorated threshold that went over two elegant white chairs for the bride and groom.

The guests were greeted by sophisticatedly dressed waiters serving appetizers.

The sit down dinner consisted of a five-course meal. While we ate, a popular Middle Eastern band played soft music. After dinner, we sat in our chairs and as every one watched, Fouad took my wedding band and switched it from the right hand to the left hand and I did the same for him. This ritual represented that we were formally married. Then, he lifted my veil and gave me a very soft and quick kiss on the lips. Right after, Rauf came around with all the boxes carrying the jewelry my husband had bought for me days before. I didn't recognize a red velvet box adorned with golden details. Fouad insisted that I open that one first. In it, were two bracelets, mabrume, traditionally given by the groom to his bride. I knew that the mabrume is considered one of the most impressive pieces of jewelry in the Middle East. This bracelet consists of strands of gold twisted to look like a thick solid piece of rope with two solid gold nuggets, one on each end. The ends don't intersect nor cross, they run parallel and barely touch each other, like cars on a two way street. This gift was poetry, a perfect description of our relationship, a forced closeness that would never come full circle.

He immediately started putting every piece on me starting with the mabrume on my wrist, moving to my fingers and then up to my neck.

As the guests lined up to give me more gold jewelry, a singer and a belly dancer joined the band livening up the party. First, I was congratulated by Fouad's three sisters: Amani, Tahani and Reejam. They were very pretty and seemed very sweet. They were all married and lived in a small town a few hours away. It was obvious that Fouad wasn't too close to them. Yet, they seemed happy that their brother was settling down. The president's wife and Rania also came to wish us well and shower me with gold. I couldn't shake the feeling that Rania was upset with this marriage. I even wondered if she had hoped to be Fouad's bride.

More women kept lining up and bringing gifts. It was overwhelming and bizarre to have total strangers placing all these pieces of gold on me. I must have had at least three rings on every finger, about 20 chains and countless bracelets and charms. Once again, all the stares and glares from mostly strangers were on me. The women surrounding me were so impressed. The single girls appeared green with envy. If they only knew, I would have given it all up in a second for my freedom. I would have been happy just marrying a simple man who loved me and whom I loved. I guess they wouldn't understand.

The guests insisted that Fouad and I dance. I wasn't too pleased with the idea but I had to act enthusiastic. Suddenly, the music went from lively to soft, from Arabic to English. They played "Endless Love." It was ironic to dance to such a beautiful, passionate song with someone who meant nothing to me. He was proud, taking me by the hand and walking me towards the dance floor. He held me close and tight, then, whispered in my ear.

"I requested this song for you. I wanted you to feel at home. Are you enjoying our evening?"

"Very much," I said politely.

"I actually can't wait to be alone with you."

The music ended and the band picked up the mood with Antarahn folk music. We probably danced for 5 minutes and then I told him I needed to sit because I was tired.

Three hours into the celebration, we cut the cake and gave our guests nicely wrapped favors with a variety of typical sweets from the region. There were sugar-covered almonds, fine chocolates with nuts packed in bright colored foil and a gelatin-like textured candy filled with pistachios.

As guests gathered on the huge terrace overlooking the Mediterranean, a fireworks display mesmerized all. It would have truly been an enchanting evening if I had married someone I actually loved.

Many, including Fouad, stayed outdoors to smoke the bubble pipe and drink coffee. The smoking of the argheele or sheesha, was a Middle Eastern pastime. Men and women alike spent hours talking, smoking and sipping coffee or tea for diversion.

An hour later, we said our goodbyes. I was saddened because I knew it was the last time I would see my father in Antarah. He was departing the next morning and I would be leaving on my honeymoon. I bowed and touched his hand with my forehead and then kissed it as a sign of respect. Tears rolled down my cheeks.

"I'll miss you, Baba," I said.

"I'll miss you too, habeebtee Fatme but your life is here, by your husband's side."

I gave him a big hug and a kiss on each cheek. He wiped my tears and gave me a kiss on the forehead.

The caravan of cabs arrived just in time to escort us around town. We led the fleet in a white limousine decorated with flowers and streamers. The custom is for the caravan to go all over the city, late at night, honking the horns to let everyone know someone just got married. I was very anxious because this indicated that soon I would be alone with Fouad. I knew he was eager for this moment to arrive and that was a terrifying thought; the beginning of my nightmare.

chapter 9

The Honeymoon

I swam for hours to forget, until the sky started to show traces of the sun breaking through. As I walked back to the room, I could still feel the pain, the raw sensation inside. I kept trying to wipe the tears with my hands and erase the horrific images from my head. He had been an animal with no regard. I wondered if this feeling would ever go away or would it get worse. I put on some dry clothes and rocked myself to sleep hoping I would wake up to discover it was just a bad dream.

When I woke up, it was so vivid. I was truly living what I wished to forget. The sound of his voice and his touch were the reminder that it was all very real.

"Saba Al Khair, good morning my darling," he said startling me then kissing my bruised neck. "I really did a number on you last night. Cover up those hickeys."

I saw a pantsuit and a matching scarf that had been laid out for me.

"I expect for you to act and dress like a lady. Wear the hijab, and long sleeves. Also, tone down your makeup. You don't need to look like a whore. You are a respectable married woman now. Beautiful just the way God made you."

"Is that supposed to be a compliment? Have I lost my entire identity to you?"

"You lost your virginity to me. Now, you are damaged goods; my goods. You are under my roof and you will follow my rules. There will be no more discussion on this matter. Get dressed. We will be picked up shortly and I hate to be late. Don't worry about packing. I've prepared a bag for you with everything you need. It is downstairs."

"Lovely," I said as I slammed the door behind him.

Our honeymoon was a guarded secret. The chauffeur picked us up and dropped us by the pier. We stepped on to a beautiful yacht and were greeted by its owner, a friendly face, Rauf. I was relieved he was going to accompany us to our final destination, which I learned, would be Cyprus Island. Both men went down to the cabin as I overheard them talk.

"So, how was your wedding night?" Rauf asked.

"It was great," Fouad responded gloating. "She was a virgin after all. I guess you win the bet." They laughed as Fouad continued "And you know these first timers can't get enough. We were at it all night. She's insatiable. What a body! She is truly a goddess."

"I insist, you are a lucky man," Rauf said.

I was furious that they were discussing my intimacies and that they had made a bet about me being a virgin. At least Rauf had faith in me. Fouad was a pig. He had no respect for me. I was truly one more medal on his jacket.

"Are you going to meet up with your Greek hottie in Cyprus?" Fouad asked.

"Melina, of course."

"I hope you told her not to bring a friend. I'm a married man now and I have to keep appearances. At least in the beginning" Fouad said as they laughed.

I felt betrayed and disappointed even by Rauf. I suspected my marriage had no future but now, I was certain I would learn to hate him every day a little more. He was a known playboy and wasn't prepared to settle down. I wasn't about to fight over him either. Actually, this was probably for the best. Maybe he would leave me alone to go after new conquests.

"How's Rania?" Fouad asked.

"Devastated."

"I'm sorry brother but I just couldn't commit to her. I knew I wouldn't make her happy and I couldn't afford the eyes of the world on me. In addition, I couldn't fulfill your father's expectations in regards to his daughter."

"That's all in the past my friend. She'll get over it. It's not as if she lacks admirers," Rauf said as he walked off heading towards the stairs.

This conversation explained Rania's strange behavior around me. Yet, I was puzzled. Rania seemed like a perfect match for him and his blind ambition. This woman could put the world at his feet together with the power and control he obviously craved. So, why me? What could he possibly gain from me?

"Eavesdropping, Fatima?" Rauf asked.

"I got bored up there so I came to see what you gentlemen were doing," I said startled as Fouad abruptly got up from his chair.

"Nothing that concerns you, dear. We will be up shortly."

Up on deck, I started to see some land at a distance. It was a gorgeous day. I unraveled my veil and let my hair blow as my mind drifted. I thought about my father and how he would cope now that neither my mother nor I were there to keep him company. I thought about my mother and how I wish I would have had more time with her. I needed her advice, her wisdom and mostly her love.

As I stared into the deep blue sea, I dared to think the unthinkable: giving up on life; just allowing myself to be swallowed slowly by the current into a peaceful abyss. Two things stopped me: fear of Allah and my father's unbearable sadness.

Suicide would be an unforgivable haram, sin, and my father could not survive another loss.

My fate had been decided and I had to learn to live with it. As I wiped my eyes, the men came up on deck. I quickly wrapped the scarf around my neck to cover those awful marks.

"Tears on a newlywed's eyes?" Rauf asked.

"No. My eyes are just sensitive to the sun and I forgot my sunglasses."

"Borrow mine," Rauf insisted.

"No need," Fouad said. "Here are your sunglasses, sweetie."

He gently pulled my hair and whispered in my ear.

"Cover your hair immediately. I thought I made it clear that I am the only man who could see your hair."

I carefully covered my head with the scarf making sure not to expose any hair to avoid an embarrassing scene in front of Rauf.

Seconds later, Fouad started acting very loving. I sensed Rauf was a little uncomfortable with this but he smiled.

"Love is a beautiful thing," Rauf said.

We had finally arrived to Cyprus.

The golden sand, the luxurious resorts, the fresh breeze and the clear water made this a true romantic paradise. I kept wondering what secrets would be revealed if these shores could talk. I wondered how many women Fouad had brought here and how many broken hearts he had left behind. I actually felt guilty knowing that Rania and probably others were suffering when I would gladly give him up for my old life.

We checked into a lavish suite overlooking the ocean. Fouad was obsessed with keeping up with appearances. Status meant everything to him. I was more interested in a simple, quiet life away from bodyguards and fake people.

When I started unpacking, I realized Fouad was making a point to buy me some extremely conservative outfits. Everything was black. Everything was long-sleeved, oversized blouses, long skirts, pants and an abaye, coat, for me to wear over the clothes. This sheer coat would guarantee I was concealing every inch of my body and of course, several black scarves to cover my hair. On the other hand, the pig managed to pack some very skimpy lingerie.

"Is this what I'm supposed to wear to the beach?" I said holding up a thong.

"Very funny" he replied.

"Why do you want to dress me like an old lady?"

"Correction: a married woman. This," he said pointing at the clothes, "is what I want to see you wear. Starting tonight I also want you to stop, as you Americans say, the 'chit-chat' with Rauf. He is not your friend. A decent married woman has no business interacting with any other man but her husband. Unless the yacht is on fire or sinking, I prohibit you to speak to him."

"Fouad, you are being unreasonable. How are you going to justify me not talking to the man when I've been doing so up till now?"

"Set the boundaries and he will follow your lead."

"Do I detect a tad bit of jealousy?"

"There is nothing to be jealous of," he said in a very arrogant tone. "You are used goods, my darling, and a man like Rauf wouldn't lay his eyes on you. If he did, I would kill him before he put a hand on you. Are we clear?"

"Crystal."

"Now, go change and model one of those sexy numbers for me." There was a knock at the door. As he went to open it, I rushed to put on my scarf. It was Rauf. Both men spoke briefly.

"Be ready for dinner. Rauf and I have some business to take care of."

I was relieved. I headed to the balcony to catch a glimpse of happiness while I watched couples that were truly in love. A few minutes later I saw Rauf and Fouad as they were greeted by two bikini bombshells that they escorted to the yacht.

I wasn't jealous, I just expected him to be discrete. After all, it was our honeymoon and he was with a high profile individual. I couldn't believe he had no problem prancing around the resort with his sharmuta. I understood then why Fouad didn't pursue Rania. The president of Antarah would never have tolerated any man making a mockery of his daughter. This would have spelled disaster for Fouad's military career.

Several hours passed and I finally went to bed. When he walked in, he tried to wake me up but I pretended to be sound asleep.

I decided to allow Fouad to go on with his rendezvous. The more time he was tied up, the less time I had to deal with him. I prayed he'd be exhausted after his active escapades and would leave me alone. Unfortunately, the bastard had enough testosterone to go around. So, I played the sleeping beauty card and avoided intercourse for a couple of nights.

It was day three and I had successfully kept my distance from Rauf and I guess he got the hint that our flirting days were over.

The honeymoon that never started was coming to an end and now reality was about to sink in. We were headed home and I was about to officially start my role as a housewife.

Married Life

The first day Fouad returned to work, I took some time to acquaint myself with the house. The most fascinating room was my husband's study because it was his sanctuary the same way it was for my father. It reflected his personality: strong, arrogant and disciplined. Everything had its place.

The walls were filled with certificates, awards, commendations and his degree from the prestigious Cranfield University in England. He was top of his class at the royal military college of science. It was actually at Shrivenham campus were he met Rauf. They were both attending a 1 year advanced education war studies program.

He claims he didn't know who Rauf was in the beginning, but knowing Fouad, it was no coincidence. I believe he strategically placed himself where he knew he would meet the president's son.

Fouad got his Masters in Defense Administration & Management. This degree together with his presidential contacts helped him move along the military ranks. With Rauf's support, he gained the president's trust and respect. Colonel Mustafa was now the assistant chief executive of the Air Force. It would take several years to move up the military ladder and become Major General, the minimum rank needed to head the Air Force. Fouad was on the right track and nothing would stop him from achieving his objective.

Rauf was being groomed to become the next president in the event of his father's death or retirement due to illness. I was sure Fouad's ultimate goal was for Rauf to appoint him his vice president. His ambition and determination could certainly earn him this position. Fouad was committed. He put in long hours, went through extensive training sessions and seminars that kept him away from home quite often. I admired his drive. Unfortunately, this wasn't enough to win me over.

It took a few weeks to settle into a routine. Jamila came to visit often and brought a splash of sunshine in to my otherwise dull days. She was starting to look very pregnant. Fouad had taken her husband Nabil under his wing in an effort to please me. In return, I started to be nicer. I used cooking as my therapy making my husband happy and my life easier.

Little by little, I started meeting other military wives, Nur andMariam were my favorites, and I realized that most of them had pre-arranged marriages. It was a concept that I could never grasp but I had learned to accept. Some of them even admitted that they had a tough time adapting to their spouse's demands and strict military ways but in the end had grown to love them. So, I joined the club. Day by day, I tried to make my life with Fouad agreeable. With my affection, I had tamed his controlling ways.

We frequently had our friends over for dinner. He constantly flattered my cooking which made me feel accomplished. He even rewarded my efforts by adding more color to my wardrobe. I felt I was one step away from taking off my scarf for good. Wishful thinking! Things were looking up. Fouad's attentiveness was starting to rub off on me. I was becoming more giving, which made even our sex life seem almost enjoyable.

Before we married, I had made a conscious decision to get on birth control behind Fouad's back. It was inconceivable to bring a child into a loveless marriage.

For months, he insisted that I see a doctor to find out if there was a problem. I tried to blame it on our irregular sexual activity because of his extended periods of absence due to his military operations. I also used my mother's problems in conceiving me as something that might be hereditary. I always insisted he be patient and put it in God's hands.

Now, I was reconsidering my position. I actually started to feel that a child would allow me to focus on something other than myself and bring meaning to my life. A child might even help me develop feelings for Fouad I never imagined possible. For the first time, I was planning a future.

When Jamila had her baby, I was by her side assisting the midwife as she pushed her bundle of joy into this world. Outside the room, an anxious Nabil awaited to hear the glorious words.

"It's a boy!" the midwife shouted.

Nabil rushed in to see his beautiful offspring for the first time. His eyes watered as he thanked God for his tiny miracle. He then turned to his wife, held her hand and kissed her forehead. It was a very tender moment.

When Jamila held her newborn in her arms, I really felt my maternal instincts kicking in. I guess Jamila saw how I melted in the presence of this adorable creature.

"Here's your nephew Ramee," she said.

As I took him in my arms, I cried. I thought about my mother and how it must have felt to have me in her arms after wanting me so much. I thought about my dad and how proud he was of me. I also remembered how his love made me conquer all my fears. Ramee was going to have a wonderful life. Two parents who loved each other and absolutely adored him and an aunt to spoil him rotten. What else could a boy need?

Nabil was sitting by Jamila's side as I walked toward him and put the baby in his arms.

"Your son is beautiful, Abu Ramee and Em Ramee," I said to the proud parents. "God bless him today and forever."

From now on, Jamila and Nabil would be known as abu, father of, and em, mother of, Ramee. Their first born son became their identity; their purpose. That's what life was all about.

They immediately discussed the traditional sacrificing of sheep; two sheep if it's a boy; one if it's a girl. It is customary to distribute the meat among the poor for Allah to bless the newborn child.

Friends and family began to arrive sharing their best wishes with the proud parents. Fouad had also come to congratulate them.

"Mabruk, Abu Ramee and Em Ramee," he said as he looked at Ramee.

"Masha Allah, what a gorgeous little fellow," he continued.

"So, I hope you guys are next," Jamila replied.

"Insha Allah," Fouad looked at me and smiled.

I was actually excited about the possibilities. What better way to start trying than our upcoming vacation. It was going to be our first wedding anniversary. Who would've known then I would have a change of heart. I was truly looking forward to it. We were going with a few other married couples, along with Rauf and his flavor of the month.

Fouad had truly turned a leaf. We were spending more time together and actually talking. He was starting to treat me as an equal listening to what I had to say. He expressed pride and respect towards me in front of others. I began to feel I could trust him. No more escapades, affairs or wandering eyes. I was convinced that he was smitten by my charms and that my feistiness was a turn on.

Fouad even warmed up to the idea of me greeting his male friends, in a respectful matter of course, and even holding a conversation in a group setting. Although most times, the men sat in Fouad's personal study and the ladies gathered around the kitchen table. The Muslim religion encourages men and women not to interact to avoid temptation. I would just enter the room to serve them a cup of shy, tea or ahwa.

Two days before our anniversary, we were going to the theater to see Romeo and Juliet. The night before the event, he brought me this great, big box. Inside was a fabulous emerald green gown, a matching scarf and matching shoes.

"Do you like them, Fatima?" he asked.

"They are beautiful."

"Not as beautiful as you."

"I love..." I whispered shocking myself as we locked lips in a passionate kiss and made love all night long.

The next day while I was getting ready for our special evening, he came from behind and placed around my neck the most opulent emerald and diamond necklace I had ever seen. He had managed to lure me into his fancy world; a world I had been brought up in and had tried so hard to escape.

"Now you look like a goddess," he said.

With every flattering word, he had succeeded in softening my hardened heart. I actually was considering the possibility that I could develop feelings for him. But it was a bit premature to express these emotions.

The phone rang and Fouad answered. After a brief conversation he told me he had to go back to the office to sign some papers.

"Why don't we meet at the theater? I'll have the driver come back for you and I'll take a taxi," he said.

"Do you have to?" I replied disappointed.

"Duty calls. But I'll be there on time. I promise."

He kissed me on the forehead and left.

The theater in the center of town was a majestic place. It was built by the Greeks around 300 B.C and extensively reworked by the Romans. The two-story auditorium included six staircases, stone walls, rows of pillars, a magnificent stage, and the orchestra. The red velvety chairs and curtains that seemed miles long were fit for royalty. I remembered, as a child, going to theaters all over the world with my father and feeling the excitement. Now, being here for the very first time, I was overwhelmed by the sense of grandeur evoked by this marvelous place.

Several hundred people were gathered outside waiting to get in. As I stepped out of the limo, all heads turned. Rauf immediately came to escort me.

"You look ravishing tonight," Rauf said.

"You're making me blush," I replied.

The crowd moved aside as the bodyguards secured the way for the president's son to walk in with me. The president and his wife were already inside sitting at their balcony. Several people we knew greeted us as we walked in.

"Has anyone seen Fouad?" I asked.

"I thought I saw him earlier," Mariam said.

I noticed that her husband tapped her slightly in a very discrete manner. I got a very uneasy feeling and tried to put it out of my mind. As we were headed to our seats, I waved to Rauf's parents. Once again, we were stopped by friends.

"Where's Fouad?" Nur asked.

"He had to stop by the office to sign some papers but he should be here any moment," I replied.

"I wanted to introduce both of you to Dr. Ibrahim Al-Kateb," Nur continued. "He recently moved back to Antarah after years in America. This is Mrs. Fatima Aziz."

I was a little distracted during the introduction. Suddenly, when I looked up, I was drawn into his eyes and lost in the echo of his deep voice. For the first time, I was totally captivated by a man. This enchanting stranger with dreamy eyes, perfect lips and bright smile had managed to stir up feelings in me I never knew existed.

As my heartbeat accelerated and my palms became sweaty, my entire body was ignited with breathtaking sensations.

Then, unexpectedly, he extended his hand. I didn't shake it. I was afraid I would walk away with him and never turn back. Who was this man who had awakened all these new feelings in me?

I was afraid that he or the others would see right through me so, I stepped back.

"Dr. Al-Kateb, I think you forget that you are not in America. In Antarah, women, especially married women, don't shake hands with men," I said in a sharp tone.

The doctor gently put his hand down.

"It was an honor to meet you," he said in a very secure voice and continued. "I apologize if I made you uncomfortable. I have to remember that here, I have to abide by the customs," he said staring at me.

Then, Dr. Al-Kateb shook hands with Rauf.

"It's been a while," Rauf said. "It's good to have you back working at the hospital. We'll have to get together."

Nur took me aside.

"You look spectacular this evening. The doctor is a cutie, isn't he?" she said.

"I'm a married woman Nur and, need I remind you, you are also. Where is Fouad? The play is about to start."

I turned to Rauf. "Are you ready?"

Rauf and I sat with an empty seat between us, Fouad's seat. I kept looking at my watch worried about Fouad and thinking about the doctor.

Rauf excused himself to go call Fouad. When he came back, he whispered in my ear that my husband had been tied up at the office but would try his best to make it before intermission.

During intermission, Rauf took me to greet his parents. We spoke briefly and I excused myself to go powder my nose. I sneaked backstage to take a quick look in a mirror. By mistake, I stumbled upon an actress' dressing room and slowly opened the door hoping it would be empty. As I opened it, I heard some thumping and some moaning.

When I looked through the mirror, I saw him. Fouad was literally caught with his pants down. He was pressing against the young starlet's naked body which he had bent over a chair. While he squeezed the side of her buttocks, he moved roughly pleasuring himself. Then, abruptly, he stopped as he caught a glimpse of me through the mirror. Immediately, I ran off. I heard him call my name while I stormed out of the theater.

As I was getting in the taxi, I looked up and at a distance saw Dr. Al- Kateb waiving good bye.

The entire trip home I kept replaying the image of Fouad and that woman. I also kept thinking about Dr. Al-Kateb. I just couldn't get him out of my mind.

When I arrived, I tried to unclasp the necklace Fouad had given me earlier. In a failed attempt and frustrated, I just pulled it off, breaking it and leaving a mark around my neck. I took my clothes off and bundled them in a bag. I was throwing things all over our bedroom. I was infuriated. A deep feeling of betrayal had consumed my body.

I went to my safe haven, the pool, to think.

As I swam, I remembered our wedding night and the humiliations he put me through time and time again. This was the Fouad I knew and hated. He had never changed. He was the same bastard I met a year ago and would always be.

Fouad arrived a few minutes later. I could hear his muffled voice in the water calling my name. I kept swimming intensely like I did in my youth during swim meets. This time, I was racing for my sanity.

"Fatima. Talk to me."

I ignored his requests.

Suddenly, I felt the thump in the water and a pull on my legs.

"Go away. I hate you," I said as I came up. "I never should have married you. I should have known a playboy like you would never settle with one woman."

He raised his hand to slap me but stopped himself. There was an almost remorseful look on his face. Enraged, I spit on his face.

"You disgust me."

Suddenly, he held me forcefully close to his body. He was aroused by my reaction. As I tried to set myself loose, he let me go. I immediately rushed to the steps, and raced to the bedroom locking the door behind me afraid he would come take me by force.

Minutes later, he was on the other side of the door.

"Forgive me, Fatima. I truly love you."

I crawled into a corner shivering as the events of the evening rushed through my mind and wondered why.

I cried myself to sleep and asked myself a million times how could I have been so stupid. Yet, in all my misery and confusion, I could not stop thinking about Dr. Ibrahim Al-Kateb and the feelings he had awoken in me.

The dreams of having a child and happily ever after were shattered. My love died before it even had a chance to blossom. Divorce was out of the question. It was his word against mine about the infidelity and there were no witnesses to back my claim. Fouad would never let me go. He would keep me a prisoner in my own home if I tried to fight this.

I woke up restless and went back to the pool to clear my mind and reflect on my future. With every breath, I released my anger and began to see an opportunity. I had to be very clever and play my cards right.

I started thinking how I would use this chain of events and his apparent remorse to manipulate Fouad into letting me do what I wanted. It was time to move into a new direction where I would set new rules. I had to play the role of the wounded bird to wrap him around my finger and take control of my life.

"The show must go on," I thought. So, after a long shower, I headed to the kitchen for some coffee. I noticed he was sleeping in one of the guestrooms. Minutes later, he was standing in front of me.

"I don't know what came over me last night…"

"I don't want to discuss what happened. Not now, not ever," I said.

"I am so sorry, Fatima. I love you," he said as he tried to hug me.

"Don't," I pulled away. "I'll be moving into one of the guestrooms."

"No. I want you to stay in our bedroom. I'll move out," he paused. "Fatima, let's go on our trip. Let's put this unfortunate episode behind us."

"Easy for you to say. I caught you screwing another woman last night. How am I supposed to erase that revolting image from my memory?"

"I'm guilty. It was an unforgivable mistake but I love you too much and I know you have a big, forgiving heart. I admit I'm weak but, I don't want to lose you."

"You just want me to pretend nothing happened; forgive and forget. How about Cyprus? You think I bought that story of Rauf and you taking care of some business on a daily basis? I saw you with that woman. And I'm sure there were others after that. But, I didn't say anything because I didn't give a damn," I paused. "Then, something happened. Little by little, we started to grow closer and I thought... I guess I was a fool to think you were capable of loving anyone other than yourself. Why Fouad? You know what? Don't even waste your breath. Forget it. I'm not going anywhere with you. I have an idea; maybe you want to ask that sharmuta you were with last night to go with you."

"That woman means nothing to me," he said raising his voice.

"She meant enough to risk losing me. This is useless. I don't want to talk about this anymore. My decision is final. I am not going."

"What are we going to tell our friends?"

"I'm sure you'll come up with the perfect excuse. Or better yet, why don't you tell them the real reason we are not going?"

Later that morning in Fouad's office...

"Hi, my dear. I miss you. I need you back in Antarah. It is time."

"Isn't it a little soon?"

"Do I detect hesitation?"

"Of course not. It was about time. I miss everything about you. I hate knowing that she is in your arms instead of me."

"It's only you I think about, Esmaa. How long will it take you to tie all lose ends and get here? I have a position waiting for you."

"The perfect position is you and me on your office desk."

"We'll have a lifetime for that my dear."

"Can't wait..."

Declaration Of Independence

During the weeks that followed, I was able to develop a plan that would bring me as close to freedom as I possibly could get.

Surprisingly, I received a call from my father. It was almost as if he sensed I was hurting, but I did not want to burden him with my problems. I led him to believe things were great between Fouad and me.

As usual, he asked about Jamila. He also wanted to know if I was blessing him with a grandchild. I painfully responded.

"No."

I would have loved to give him the joyous news he longed to hear but now more than ever it was impossible.

Baba informed me that he was leasing our home and moving to the infamous Watergate Apartments. He felt the house was too big for him especially now that Samira wanted to move back to Antarah. He was also surrounded by too many painful memories.

I asked my father to convince Samira to move into my house to help me with the cooking and the chores. I needed an ally; someone I could trust with my life. I knew she loved me like a daughter and would be loyal. She immediately agreed.

I started contacting my closer friends feeding them the line that I felt down and lonely. I told them Fouad worked such long hours and was away so much that I was going crazy. Jamila, unaware of my situation, suggested I should have a baby. She joked that I was going through a postpartum depression even though she was the one who had the baby.

I insisted that I needed a challenge in my life and motherhood was not the answer. I reminded her about that speech she once gave me about making a difference for the people of Antarah. I spoke to Nur and Mariam about my education and my desire for an outlet to express my talents. In a subtle way, I was getting them to intercede on my behalf.

Finally, a few weeks later, Jamila, Nur and Mariam went by Fouad's office.

"Ladies, what a surprise," he said. "Where's my little Ramee?

"He is actually with Fatima," Jamila said. "I told her I needed to run some errands and I thought she could use Ramee's charm to cheer her up."

"Fatima doesn't know we are here," Nur replied.

"We came because we are worried about her," Jamila explained. "She hasn't been herself lately. She seems depressed."

"So, what do you suggest I do?" he said in a semi sarcastic tone.

"She needs a distraction," Mariam answered.

"I've tried to convince her to go visit her father in Washington or go with me on a romantic getaway," he insisted.

"We're talking about a more permanent distraction," Nur said.

"What do you mean?" he curiously replied.

"Well, she has a degree in psychology with a minor in anthropology. I know she had planned to go for her Masters' in social work, " Jamila answered. "The hospital is short handed. It could really use her skills."

"A job," he paused. "Did she put you up to this?"

"No. She knows nothing about it and we rather you not tell her we were here. The hospital is looking for volunteers to work with children. She's mentioned her desire to start a family. This opportunity could be very inspiring," Nur added.

"Who will take care of the house?' he asked concerned.

"Khale Samira is moving back to Antarah. I'm sure she would love to help Fatima with her house duties," Jamila replied.

"Anyway the position is part-time so she wouldn't be out all day," Mariam added.

"All this is very unexpected. I'll have to give it some serious consideration and discuss it with Fatima," he said.

"I hope we didn't overstep by coming to see you," Jamila said.

"Ladies, it was a pleasure. I appreciate your concern for my wife. I'm pleased to know she has such good friends. My regards to Abu Ramee and kiss that beautiful boy of yours on his uncle's behalf," he said.

"Masalame, God be with you, Fouad," the ladies said.

"Allah isalmec, God be with you," he replied.

When he got home that evening, he called me into his study.

"Fatima, we have to talk. I feel I've given you enough space. I'm concerned about you," he said as he tried to caress me.

I pulled back and sat down.

"I heard Samira is moving back to Antarah,"

"Did you speak to Baba?" I asked.

"No."

"So, who told you?"

"That's not important. Have you told anyone about us?"

"No."

"Not even Jamila?"

I knew he was fishing. "No. You think I take pleasure degrading myself? Fouad, what's this about?"

"It's about a truce."

"If it's another trip, I'm not interested."

"How would you like to volunteer at the hospital working with children?" he said.

The children angle did the trick; he truly felt this would push me to want to start a family.

"You're kidding, right? You, allowing me to spend time outside the house in a working environment?"

"You've earned my trust. I want to see you smiling again. I want us to recapture what we once had. One of us has to give in. It's only fair for it to be me. I want to make up for my mistakes. I owe it to you," he said.

The olive branch had officially been extended. He was almost believable with his noble gesture. Unfortunately, faithfulness was an unreachable goal. I had to be realistic and follow through with my plan.

"I'll have to think about it, Fouad. The only thing I know for sure is that I want Samira to come live with us. She could keep me company especially when you go on your trips."

"That's fine. You have my support whatever you decide," he said holding my hands. "Fatima, when can I move back into our bedroom?"

"So, that's what this is all about?" I said, as I abruptly removed my hands from his.

"No. It's about you and our love, and how much I miss you."

I desperately wanted to believe in him but I knew he could not be trusted. Everything was going according to my plans. It was best for me to let him in my bed after the position at the hospital was a done deal. If not, he might change his mind. I needed leverage and the only tool I had at my disposal was sex.

A few days later, I organized a dinner party. I invited Jamila and Nabil together with Nur, Mariam and their husbands, and a few of Fouad's colleagues and their wives, Nessreen and Manar, who were new to our small group. They seemed to be very nice ladies and I had no problem expanding my circle of friends. Fouad was very thrilled to see his old Fatima back. I looked great and felt even better. My friends were shocked to see me in such good spirits.

"I'm going to be having competition in the kitchen pretty soon. Samira, Jamila's aunt, is leaving Washington and coming to live with us. She's the best. She's like a mother to me. She taught Jamila and me everything we know about cooking."

"Jamila always told me no one can cook like her Khale Samira," Nabil replied. "I'm actually jealous she won't be coming to live with us."

"So, that's why you're in such a fabulous mood," Nur stated.

"Well, that and the fact that I'll be volunteering at the hospital," I said.

Fouad stopped eating and looked up at me.

"Yes, I suggested that Fatima take on a new challenge. I'm certain pediatrics could benefit from her skills and knowledge. I'm very proud of her," Fouad said. "Thanks, sweetheart."

Everything was running smoothly.

"I'm so happy for you, Fatima. We were starting to get worried about you," Mariam said.

"Don't be silly. You know we all have are ups and downs. I was just feeling a little lonely with Fouad's crazy schedule: one week home, three weeks in the field. The life of a military wife isn't easy. I haven't gotten used to Fouad being away from me for so long."

What a performance, and Fouad was buying into every word.

"I know what you're saying. I still can't get used to it after five years of marriage," Manar said.

"Well, someone has to make the money to keep you ladies living like queens," said Manar's husband Muhammad as the men laughed.

"The evening was a true success," Fouad said as he kissed my neck from behind. "You caught me off guard with the volunteering news. I thought you wanted to think it through."

"I did. I knew I had your support so I shared. You are not changing your mind, are you?"

"Of course not, on the contrary, I'm happy for you," he said holding my chin up with his hand. "Let me taste your lips again, Fatima."

As we kissed, I felt he was getting aroused, so I stopped him.

"I need more time. Good night, Fouad."

I was truly expecting the monster from our first night to re-appear and force himself on me but he accepted my request. I still had feelings for him but I was sickened by the images of him with other women. Although he seemed regretful, there was no guarantee that he was not sleeping around.

A week later, Samira arrived to the house. I was pleased that she and Fouad got along from the start.

Every morning, Samira left, before sunrise, to pick up the piping hot pita bread from the bakery. When she brought it home, it was still puffy. After breakfast, she went to the market to buy all the fresh ingredients for that day's meal. It was one of the perks of living in Antarah; nothing but the freshest vegetables, meat, fish and fruit.

Every item was hand picked. Homemade dairy products were delivered to our door from the countryside every few days. Seasonal items were purchased once every six months and stored in the pantry to be used year round.

While Fouad was delighted with her cooking, I was ecstatic with the idea of starting a new chapter in my life.

chapter 12

A Refreshing Surprise

Monday morning I went to the hospital. After the head of personnel reviewed my credentials, I was offered a job as a social worker in pediatrics. They were understaffed and in desperate need for help. I explained I could only work part-time. I was taking a chance accepting this kind of responsibility without Fouad's consent but I was not planning to tell him about being promoted from volunteer to employee; at least not yet.

Dalal, the head nurse in pediatrics introduced me to the staff. One of the doctors was with a patient. When the patient left, she walked in with me.

"Good morning, doctor," Dalal said.

His back was to us. He was filling out a chart. "One moment," he said.

"I just wanted to introduce you to our new social worker."

When he turned, I froze.

"Hello, Mrs. Aziz. Welcome to our team," he said.

"You two know each other?"

At once, I said "No," while he said "Yes."

"Don't you remember? Your friend Nur Adra introduced us. Dr. Ibrahim Al-Kateb at your service. I won't attempt to shake your hand this time, but it is great seeing you again."

"Oh, how foolish of me. Yes, Romeo and Juliet at the theater. How could I forget?"

"Nurse Dalal, the patient in Room 303 is asking for you," an orderly said.

"Excuse me, doctor. Fatima, you're in good hands," she said rushing out.

I wanted the earth to swallow me. I remembered exactly who he was. I remembered exactly how he made me feel. But, I could not let on that his face had been imprinted in my memory since the day we met. I was like a schoolgirl with a crush. I'm sure I was blushing.

"Did you ever find your husband that night?" he asked.

"What do you mean?" I replied a little edgy.

"I'm sorry. I didn't mean to pry but I remember you were distracted asking Nur if she had seen him."

"You remember more about that night than I do and to answer your question, yes, I found him."

"So, did you like the play?"

"It was nice."

"Why did you leave during intermission? I saw you taking a cab."

"It was some kind of minor emergency. It's been a while. I really can't remember."

I wanted to forget that awful night. Yet, I was curious to know why Dr. Ibrahim remembered every detail.

"You looked stunning that evening," he said.

"Dr. Al-Kateb, I don't think your wife would appreciate such flattery

towards another woman."

"My wife died over a year ago but she would have agreed that you are a beautiful woman. She never understood why I married an American girl. She felt the Middle East had the most exquisite looking women in the world."

"I'm so sorry about your wife."

"It was a real tragedy but I had to move on with my life to honor hers," he replied with sadness in his voice.

"You can call me Fatima, doctor," I said extending my hand.

"Ibrahim," he said as he reached out to shake mine.

It felt like a jolt of electricity ran throughout my body. His handshake was confident. His hands were strong yet soft, the hands of a healer.

After a few seconds, I slipped my hand from his. I was afraid of my feelings. I was so vulnerable because of my situation with Fouad that I didn't want to confuse my heart.

"Well, I better get going," I said.

"I'm sure I'll be seeing you around."

I thought about Ibrahim all day. When I got home that evening, I was greeted with flowers and a candle lit dinner.

"You really out did yourself," I said.

"How was your first day at the hospital?" Fouad asked.

"It was great. The people are friendly and kind. I'm surrounded by children. It's wonderful."

"Any men I should worry about?" he asked.

"It's not an all women's hospital. Besides, you know you can trust me," I replied as I rubbed his shoulders.

"I do. Your hands on my shoulders feel great, just press a little harder. Yes, that's the spot. Thanks, Fatima."

In reality, there was a man. A man I had not been able to get out of my mind since the first time I met him. But, I had to keep up my farce. That night, I invited Fouad back into our bedroom. We made love but it wasn't the same. My body was there but my mind was somewhere else. I felt as empty as our first time.

At the hospital, I had a small office. It was great to have a place of my own; a place to think. I met with several nurses and doctors to get some feedback on our patients and their needs. We had some terminally ill children with parents who needed support and guidance.

My first order of business was to develop a preventative program to help keep the children of Antarah physically and emotionally healthy.

I loved my job but, I must confess, Ibrahim had become one of the major reasons I looked forward to going to work. I saw him almost every day. We did not talk much because he had a heavy patient load and he spent many hours in surgery. When we did see each other, we just made small talk.

Once a week pediatrics held meetings to exchange ideas, discuss problems and report headway in our department. In one of those meetings, Dr. Al-Kateb brought up the desperate need to disseminate information to parents about immunizing their children.

After the meeting, I approached him about working together on an immunization awareness campaign. He was thrilled with the idea. I was delighted to sink my teeth into a project that would make a difference and would earn me his respect.

The timing was ideal. Fouad was going with Rauf on a business trip for a couple of weeks, so it was the perfect opportunity to throw myself into my work without distractions.

With Fouad gone, I was much more relaxed and put full days at the hospital. I instructed Samira to make excuses if my husband called asking for me. Under no circumstance, did I want him to know that work was taking up my days.

"I have a surprise for you," Ibrahim said.

"What is it?"

"Today we are going to some less fortunate neighborhoods to vaccinate the children. You will see the working conditions and hopefully you can come up with some ideas on how to improve what we have."

"I'm ready. Will Dalal be joining us?"

"As far as I know, yes."

I felt it was not appropriate for the good doctor and me to be left alone; too many eyes watching and too much room for misinterpretations. Dalal had become a good friend and I felt very comfortable around her.

We went downstairs with a few boxes of supplies. Waiting for us was a beat up van equipped with a loud speaker. We drove around the neighborhoods alerting the people that we would be in the area taking care of the children's shots.

Then, we parked the vehicle and waited for the children to come. If the turnout was weak, we stepped out of the van and approached people directly. We tried to make the parents aware of the importance of vaccines.

It was an uphill battle. We made it possible for the children to stay healthy yet, the parents did not cooperate. They felt it was not necessary. They were more concerned with coming up with the money for their next meal.

I was faced with Antarah's reality; extreme poverty. There were no jobs, no hope. The rich were getting wealthier and the poor seemed to be deprived of their basic needs.

As we handed out aspirin and over the counter medications that we brought to distribute among the elderly, I asked myself, "What can I do to bring a spark of hope to these people?"

We needed to modernize our equipment and establish a closer relationship with the community. We had to earn their trust, to educate them on preventative measures and to keep their children and themselves healthy. This task would be challenging, but with Dr. Al- Kateb's support, I was certain we could improve the people's health care.

Several months had passed. I had neglected my friends and my little Ramee. Maybe Ramee reminded me of what I wanted and could not have. I promised to spoil him and love him unconditionally and I was not doing that great of a job.

Dalal and I had grown closer because we spent so much time together. When I met her, she was a newlywed. Now, she was ready to give birth to her first child. I wanted to do something special for her so, I convinced Fouad to let me throw her a surprise baby shower.

This was unheard of in Antarah but it was an American custom that I felt the ladies would enjoy. They would all bring their children, their motherhood tips and advice and I could play host and have some fun.

I invited close to fifteen women and told them to bring along other girlfriends. It was probably thirty of us. We let our hair down, literally, because there were no men around. We listened to Arabic music and danced. Jamila and I showed off our belly dancing skills, as taught by Mama. We laughed so hard, it felt like the good old days. The days I had no cares in the world.

Dalal finally arrived. She was so excited, I thought she would go into labor in the living room. I told everyone that the custom was for the ladies to bring a baby gift. Something the mother would probably need for her newborn.

I guess it was the newness of it all but, the ladies went all out. Dalal was very thankful because these were things she would otherwise not have been able to afford.

Samira outdid herself with the food. She made our favorite Arabic and American dishes. We ordered a huge cake decorated with pink and blue baby rattles on a mint green background. We ate, danced and talked until our hearts were content.

I was very intrigued with one of the guests who didn't fit the cookie cutter mold. She came in with no scarf and wearing tight jeans, a turtle neck sweater, a leather jacket and leather ankle boots. She had a very fashionable short haircut with some blonde highlights and a distinctive fragrance, a mixture of sandalwood and vanilla.

"Hi. I'm Fatima. Welcome to my home," I said.

"Fatima, I've heard so much about you. You have a lovely place," she replied.

"Are you a friend of Dalal's?"

"Yes. I'm actually her sister-in-law, Esmaa" she said as she twirled her ring with her thumb.

"Engaged?" I asked looking at the ring on her right hand.

"God no!" she replied relieved. "I don't want a man to tell me what to do, what to wear. I'm happy the way I am. I really don't have time for anyone. My work is very consuming and I like it that way."

Her life started to sound better than mine. No one to take into account, total freedom to do what she wanted, and no strings attached…Esmaa was striking; not beautiful in the traditional sense of the word, but alluring in a self- confident, self-possessed way.

"So, what do you do, Esmaa?" I asked.

"I just arrived from Louisiana."

"The U.S."

"Last time I checked." She chuckled. "I'm a nuclear and civil engineer. I helped in the design of the external tank for the space shuttle."

"You work for NASA," I replied. "I'm impressed. What are you doing here? Just visiting I suppose."

"Actually, the company I worked for is subcontracted by NASA. Recently, I was recruited by Antarah's government to work with their weapons division," she answered. "The money is good and the opportunity is more challenging. Besides, I had nothing keeping me in the U.S."

The first thing that came to my mind were all the poor people of Antarah struggling to put food on their tables and the government spending its money foolishly developing weapons to help us kill each other. It was disappointing to live in a world where the value of human life was reduced to greed and the pursuit of power.

Suddenly, I was tapped on the shoulder.

"So, should Dalal open the gifts?" Nur asked.

"Sure," I said turning my head, then back to Esmaa. "Well, it was great meeting you. Good luck with your new job and don't be a stranger."

As Dalal opened her gifts, I remembered how she had told me about a sister-in-law that lived in America that had made her life a living hell and had almost broken up her marriage before it even started. I hoped the riff between them had been buried because Dalal was too happy to have her life turned upside down by Esmaa.

Days later, I heard from Esmaa. She called me at the hospital. She said she wanted to pass by to have a cup of tea and talk.

We met in my office.

"I really wanted to speak to someone who could relate to me," Esmaa confessed as she continued in English. "The transition is a bit harder than I anticipated. The men of Antarah aren't ready for a strong, independent woman like me. How did you ever adapt?"

"My situation was very different. You're here by choice. I had no other option. I came to Antarah to get married. Believe me, if I had to do it all over again, I would probably not be here today."

"But, you have a perfect life; a gorgeous house, great friends. I understand that you have a husband who adores you and is very powerful and influential and you even have a career. What else can you want?"

"I guess I can't complain," I responded. It was not the time to get too personal with a total stranger. "Who have you been talking to?" I was curious.

"Rauf. Who else? He was the one who suggested that I contact you. He speaks very highly of you. If I didn't know better, I'd think he has a little crush on you."

"Rauf is a good man. Are you interested in him?" I asked.

"Who wouldn't be? He's single, handsome and the president's son. What's not to like? But, I know I'm not his type. He goes for the damsel in distress kind. I'm too strong and opinionated for the Presidential Palace. Besides, marriage is the farthest thing on my mind. My career comes first."

"Have you met my husband?" I inquired.

"I haven't had the pleasure but Rauf has told me all about him." She started twirling her ring which I found quite annoying. "They've been friends since college, right?"

"Yes."

"Well, I've taken enough of your time and I have to head back to the base."

"The visit was too short. We have to do this again," I insisted.

I really hadn't made up my mind about her. I was influenced by what I knew through Dalal, yet, she was an enigma that piqued my curiosity. I wondered if the liberated, self-sufficient woman she appeared to be was only an act. Her life was what I imagined mine could have been.

chapter **13**

Second Chances

A month later, I met Esmaa at the military base. It was a holiday. We were celebrating Antarah's Independence Day with a big parade. There was an air show followed by marching troops, tanks and other military vehicles with armed soldiers. Fouad was sitting up front with the President, Rauf and their entourage. I sat a few rows back with Jamila, Nur, Mariam and Esmaa. This kind of event wasn't my idea of fun, but I had to show my support because above all, I was a military wife.

It was truly a beautiful day; not a cloud in the sky. A half-hour into the activity, Rauf came to greet us. Suddenly, we heard shots. It was chaotic. Rauf ordered us to duck to avoid any stray bullets. As he rushed to his father's side, we could see people running and screaming. More shots were heard.

By then, the president was safe in his vehicle and two other men escorted Rauf into a car.

At this point, I hurried toward the front seats looking for Fouad. Several of the president's bodyguards were dead on the floor. Fouad was also on the floor. For a moment, I thought he was dead. I was overcome by this big emptiness. It was surreal watching a man like him vulnerable.

Esmaa helped me snap out of it.

"He's been shot in the shoulder and has lost a lot of blood," she hollered.

I kneeled down quickly. Instinctively, I took my scarf and started to wrap it around his shoulder applying pressure to stop the bleeding. After I finished, I held him in my arms.

"Where's the ambulance?" I screamed hysterically.

Jamila, Nur and Mariam ran by my side to see what had happened. They were also concerned about their husbands who were participating in the event. A group of soldiers surrounded the area. They informed us that everyone else was safe.

"It was an attempt on the president's life. This man is a hero. He saved the president," the soldier affirmed with pride as he looked at Fouad.

Within a few minutes, the ambulance pulled up and I rode with Fouad as we headed to the hospital.

"Are you all right?" I asked.

"I'll survive," he replied.

"I've never been this scared in my life," I confessed.

"Were you afraid of losing me?" he asked as the ambulance doors opened.

He was rushed to the operating room to extract the bullet. I waited patiently. The ladies arrived shortly after to give their support. Rauf got to the hospital right after with the men.

"He saved my father's life. We will always be indebted to him," Rauf expressed containing his emotions.

"How is your father?"

"A little shaken and shocked that something like this could happen."

"Did they catch the person who did this?" Esmaa asked agitated.

"Yes, the shooter was shot on the spot. We've also apprehended a few men for questioning. We will get to the bottom of this. This kind of action will not be tolerated and anyone involved will be executed," he replied with a sturdy voice.

Rauf kept discussing the day's incident as I stepped out to get water. As I returned, I came across Dr. Ibrahim.

"I was looking for you. I heard what happened and came to see how you were doing. How's your husband?"

"He's in the O.R. with a bullet in his shoulder. Can you check on his status?"

"Of course, I'll be right back."

A few minutes later, he returned.

"The prognosis is good, he's in recovery."

"That's great news," Rauf sighed as he approached us.

"You'll be able to see him in about an hour. He's still under the effects of the anesthesia."

"Rauf," Dr. Ibrahim said as he hugged him and kissed him on each cheek. "How's your father?"

"Alive thanks to Fouad."

"Aljamda Allah, thank God." He turned to me. "Well, I need to get back to work but if you need anything just let me know."

Dr. Ibrahim was a good man and friend. His presence made me feel safe and reassured. When the hour was up, Rauf and I went to see Fouad.

"How are you feeling?" I asked.

"I'm fine. There is nothing to be concerned about. It comes with the job," he said. "Rauf, how's the president?"

"Alive thanks to you," Rauf said relieved. "He's called me twice to ask about you."

"Tell the president it was an honor and my duty to take a bullet for him. I would do it again if I had to."

"Thanks, brother," Rauf said while squeezing his hand.

"Fatima, let Rauf take you home, I'll be all right. "

"I want to spend the night by your side," I pleaded.

"Go home and rest. You can come see me tomorrow morning," he insisted.

"You're a stubborn man. I'll be here early in the morning. Call me if you need anything, no matter what time it is," I said as I kissed his forehead.

Rauf insisted on buying me a cup of tea before going home. Afterwards, I told him that I wanted to check in on Fouad one last time.

From the hallway, I looked through the glass into his room to see if he was asleep. To my surprise, I saw Esmaa in his room. She was holding his hand and talking to him. I was stunned.

I couldn't understand why Esmaa hadn't told me she knew Fouad. Why was she holding his hand while he laid in a hospital bed? Too many things were going through my mind. Now, wasn't the time or place to make a scene. Instead, I turned away and looked for answers somewhere else.

"So, how was the patient?" Rauf asked. "Sleeping like a baby."

I engaged in some small talk and then I started talking about Esmaa.

"Does Esmaa know Fouad?" I asked.

"Know him? Esmaa has been working in Fouad's department for the past month. They are actually putting together a weapons seminar," he said.

"Sounds interesting. How long have you known her?"

"Not very long, but I know people who know her very well and speak highly of her qualifications."

"How about as a person?"

"What's with all the questions?"

"Nothing. She's been trying to befriend me and I just want to make sure she is sincere."

"I think both of you have a lot in common. You are intelligent women, educated in the United States, trying to adapt to this country with another set of values and customs. I think she's looking for a familiar face and you are it," Rauf insisted.

"I guess you are right. I actually like her," I said as I kept playing the image of her and Fouad in that room over and over again in my mind.

The next morning, I headed to the hospital. I spoke to the doctor in charge of his case who assured me that everything was fine and that Fouad would be heading home in a couple of days.

As I walked towards his room, I realized the whole floor was swarming with secret service. The president was in the room visiting Fouad.

"Come in, my dear Fatima." He shook my hand respectfully. "You are married to a brave man. I owe him my life. You should be proud of your husband."

"Thank you, Mr. President. I am very proud of him and very grateful to Allah that you are both alive."

After a brief visit, everyone left and I stayed alone with Fouad. I had brought him the local newspapers and showed him the articles.

"So, how does it feel to be a hero?"

"I'm just a military man doing his duty."

"Don't be modest, it doesn't become you."

"So, were you afraid I would die?"

"Of course I was."

"Come closer, give your hero a kiss," he said in a naughty tone. We kissed. He was getting aroused.

"You need your rest," I said as I pulled back.

I was happy he was alive but I just couldn't shake the feeling that something was going on between Esmaa and my husband.

"So," I asked. "How long have you known Esmaa?"

"Esmaa Al-Basheer?"

"Yes."

"I guess since she moved back to Antarah. Esmaa works for me. I've actually wanted you to meet. I thought you could help her with the transition given the fact that you went through an adapting process when you got here."

"How thoughtful, but I already know Esmaa. She was at our house for Dalal's baby shower. I've met her a couple of times for tea. We were sitting together yesterday when you got shot."

"She never told me; maybe because we just discuss business at work. Actually, Esmaa came to visit me yesterday after you left. She wanted to know how I was doing."

"I know. I came back to say good night and I saw her."

"Why didn't you come in? Jealous?"

"Don't be silly. Even though I probably should be. She was holding your hand and you don't exactly have the best track record..."

"Fatima, are you ever going to trust me again? It was just a gesture of friendship."

"I'm sorry, Fouad. This conversation will have to wait till you get home."

"My relationship with Esmaa is strictly professional."

"I want to believe you."

I kissed him goodbye and told him I would be doing some paperwork at my office and would come back to see him later.

As I headed out, Rauf came to visit Fouad.

I turned around and discretely came close to the door to eavesdrop but the voices were muffled.

"How are you doing today, Fouad?" Rauf asked.

"Rauf, under no circumstance are you to tell Fatima that Esmaa and I dated years ago."

"She was asking me too many questions about Esmaa last night," Rauf said.

"Did you tell her anything?"

"Just that you work together but nothing about your past."

"Good. She saw Esmaa here last night and was asking me questions this morning. I was able to smooth things over but I can't afford more jealous rages."

"How are things between you and Esmaa?" Rauf asked with curiosity.

"You know Esmaa means the world to me, but I'm a married man now and that boat has sailed."

"I never thought I'd hear you say that."

At my office, I went through my messages. When I was leaving, I saw Dr. Ibrahim. His jolly disposition put a smile on my face.

"Your husband must be better," he said.

"Yes. Thanks for caring. I know we have to start working on our project. I just need some time," I said.

"Work can wait. Take all the time you need to take care of your husband."

"Thanks. I just need to catch up on a few things while he's in the hospital."

"Don't work too hard."

Esmaa was still on my mind. I wouldn't be at ease until I spoke to her. So, I asked her to come to the house for coffee and she agreed.

We started with the usual chit-chat and then I got down to business.

"Why didn't you tell me you knew my husband?"

"I was going to tell you the day of the parade, but with all the commotion, I didn't have a chance," Esmaa said.

"I'm just surprised you didn't call me before that day to tell me."

"Why would I?"

"It just seems odd because we've brought Fouad up so many times in our conversations and now, I find out you've been working with him for some time and neither one of you has mentioned it. Don't you find that a bit odd?"

"No. Are you upset?" Esmaa asked concerned.

"Disappointed. I saw you holding his hand at the hospital. Wouldn't that strike you as being a little bizarre if you were in my shoes?"

"Never crossed my mind. I guess because our relationship is strictly professional."

"Those were Fouad's same words."

"Fatima, I don't want to get personal but I've heard that Fouad and you have been having issues because of his flirtatious nature," Esmaa continued. "I felt uncomfortable discussing him with you. I didn't want you to see me as a threat. I don't know many people in Antarah and I value your friendship. I was trying to avoid misunderstandings. Forgive me if I didn't handle the situation properly."

"No matter what you've heard, Fouad and I are very committed to our marriage. I don't consider you, or anyone else for that matter, a threat. You still haven't told me why you were in his room after visiting hours."

"I was concerned about him. We work together. I see him almost every day. I consider him a friend. I got carried away with my emotions because of what had happened. He could have died. I just held his hand as a gesture of support. I apologize for any misinterpretation. I was just trying to be a friend to both of you."

"Maybe you've been away for too long but in Antarah married men cannot be friends with women or vice versa. Keep your hands to yourself and your distance from my husband. And, no more secrets if you want us to remain friends."

Esmaa got up and gave me a hug. It was very awkward and uncomfortable.

"Let's start with a clean slate," she said.

"Sure."

Her story wasn't totally convincing. I knew she could be trouble based on Dalal's experience. She was not to be trusted and I had to keep a close eye on her.

At this point, I had to consider her an adversary.

After a week, Fouad was released from the hospital. I was relieved to have him back home. I hoped everything was going to get back to normal now. I took some time off to pamper him. I changed his bandages and kept track of his medication. I trusted he knew I was grateful that he was alive.

It was difficult for me to pour my heart out to him and express my feelings. A lot of promises had been broken in the past and a lot of trust had been lost. I felt God was giving us a second chance and maybe it was time for me to forgive Fouad.

A few days later, he started getting back into his routine. He spent countless hours in his study working on his computer and talking on the phone. He was anxious to go back to work, but I insisted that the doctors wanted him to take it easy. I guess he felt guilty that he was neglecting me. I was actually surprised when he encouraged me to continue my work at the hospital.

I understood he had a lot on his mind and many work-related responsibilities that he felt needed his attention. Hence, I took his advice and returned to work.

chapter 14

Making a Difference

I really had abandoned my projects and needed to get back on track. I also missed seeing Dr. Ibrahim. He was a breath of fresh air. He made me forget all my disappointments during the brief moments we spent together. Something about him was so undeniably attractive. Maybe the fact that our relationship was platonic and would never go further than flirtation was what made it plain, simple fun.

Dr. Ibrahim and I did have a lot in common, especially our love for children and our desire to help the less fortunate. I never felt that connection with Fouad even when we were at our best. Fouad had two totally different sides to his personality; he could be cruel and ruthless or loving and tender. Dr. Ibrahim, on the other hand, was exactly as he appeared to be: a kind, good-natured person who wanted to make a difference.

As I entered his office, I found him kneeling on the floor doing zuher, noon prayer. He was almost finished, so I waited. I was glad to know he was a religious man in addition to all his other wonderful qualities.

"Sorry for the interruption. I didn't realize you followed the prayer times," I said.

He folded his msalaeeh, a customary, small rug used strictly for prayer, and placed it in a drawer.

"I try the best I can, although sometimes I'm in surgery." He paused. "I'm surprised to see you back so soon."

"So you're not happy to see me," I answered.

"No. I mean yes, I'm happy to see you. I just didn't expect to see you so soon. I assume you're husband is doing well?"

"Yes, he's recuperating nicely. He actually told me to come back to work. So, here I am and I have some great ideas. Got a few minutes?"

"Of course."

We went to my office and I started to share my ideas with him.

"Ever since the day we went to immunize the children, I've been thinking of ways to improve our health program. First of all, we need new vans to function as mobile units in deserted areas. We also need to open small neighborhood clinics in locations far away from the main hospitals. People need to know that they have medical options; we need to be accessible to them and their children. We need to prevent illnesses and detect health problems before it's too late," I stated enthusiastically.

"Your ideas are great, but how are we going to get the money to implement these programs?" he asked.

"We use the opportunities life gives us. The president is indebted to my husband; my father is a good friend of the president. That will get us in the door. You and I will meet with President Saeed to pitch him a detailed proposal on the vans and clinics. We will also include the idea for a fundraiser that will attract Antarah's elite. Between the government and community funds, we should be able to begin our projects. Each year, we could hold the fundraiser to upgrade our facilities. What do you think?"

"I think you are not only a beautiful woman, but also a brilliant one. Count me in."

"Can you put together a list of the towns that are in most need of a clinic and a list of doctors and nurses willing to volunteer at these clinics? Also, the number of vans we need to get the job done."

"I'll work with Dalal to get you all this information. I'm sure many of my colleagues will contribute good ideas to shape our proposal and will gladly volunteer some of their time for the less fortunate."

I was so excited that I jumped out of my chair and, spontaneously, hugged Dr. Ibrahim.

"Thanks," I said.

I saw the surprise in his face and quickly pulled away embarrassed by my actions.

When I got home that afternoon, I was tempted to tell Fouad about my plans but I was afraid he would discourage them. This was something I was very passionate about and wanted to accomplish on my own. Fouad was leaving town in a few weeks and that would give me enough time to get everything together. Still, I wanted to share my ideas with someone, so I called my father who offered his help and support if needed. While Fouad was recuperating, I surprised him by bringing Ramee to stay with us for a few days. I felt some distance between us. Maybe we were so caught up in our work that we forgot to make time for each other. Ramee's presence made us slow down and spend some time together. Fouad was thrilled with the baby. It was so nice to imagine him as a father and me as a mother. We were happy, yet I could not pin-point what was different between us.

Exactly three weeks after the shooting, we were invited to the Presidential Palace for an official ceremony. Fouad was still using a sling on his left arm. All the heads of government were there. All members of Fouad's department were also in attendance including Esmaa. At this event, Fouad was presented with a Medal of Honor. He listened as the president praised his skills and bravery.

"Antarah is a better place because of Colonel Mustafa. The Colonel exemplifies all the virtues of a great soldier. I am honored to present him with this medal," the president said.

I was very proud of his accomplishments. This was not only a distinction, but also most likely a promotion in rank that would put him a step closer to his goal. Fouad was the center of attention surrounded by the president and the rest of the V.I.P.'s. It would be a while so, I excused myself from the activity and rushed home. I then told Samira to go spend a few days with Jamila so I could have the house all to myself and prepare a special evening for my husband. I wanted to put an end to the strain between us. The way to do it was cooking some of his favorite dishes and filling our bedroom with candles and incense. Some new, sexy lingerie would also dazzle him. Now, I waited patiently for his arrival.

Fouad was finally home. I lured him with a note to our bedroom. It was dark. The candles and the incense were lit. There was soft, Arabic music playing.

"Fatima, where are you? What's all this?"

"Do you like it?"

"Very much."

"I thought we could start with dessert."

I proceeded to unbutton his shirt and take it off slowly. When I uncovered his left shoulder, I could see the fresh scar where the bullet had penetrated. I kissed it softly.

"Does it hurt? I asked concerned.

"No," he whispered as he turned to kiss me.

Then, he took me in his arms, bit my lips forcefully, and stroked every inch of my body. He was rough, like an animal in heat. We hadn't been intimate since before his accident, which explained his desperation to make me his. It wasn't as romantic as I envisioned it to be, but he was pleased and hopefully we were back on track.

"I'm famished," he said, when we were finished.

"I made all your favorites," I replied. "We are celebrating today's distinction and your promising future. How did it feel to be honored by the president with all of Antarah's cream of the crop present?"

"It was as great as what just happened between us," he said, caressing my hair.

"Well, well, don't hold back," I said jokingly. Then I paused and got serious. "Fouad, I want to give us a second chance."

"I'd like that sweetheart," he said as he kissed my neck forgetting about food and engaging my attention elsewhere.

The next day I woke up bright and early. Fouad and I had breakfast together. I was energized, ready to take on the world.

"Are you sure you have to go?" Fouad said.

"Yes, my love. But I'll be back soon."

We kissed and I headed to the hospital. When I got to the office, I realized I had left the outline for my proposal at home. I had to go back to get it. I thought I would surprise Fouad and maybe distract him for a couple of hours.

I got home and was very quiet. I wanted to surprise him. The door to Fouad's study was half way open. I could hear his voice. He was probably on the phone. I also recognized a familiar scent, a mixture of sandalwood and vanilla.

"I wanted you to be the first to know. I just hung up with the president. I've been promoted to Major General," Fouad said.

"Mabruk, congratulations!"

As I discretely looked in, I saw Esmaa. She was sitting on Fouad's lap as he unbuttoned her shirt.

"Oh baby, I've missed you. These weeks without you have been torture," he said.

"I've missed you too, Major General. When are you expecting that twit to come home?" Esmaa asked.

"Fatima?"

"Who else?"

"I don't expect her till this afternoon."

"That gives us more than enough time to burn up some calories and build up an appetite," she laughed. "Fouad, why do you stay with her? She's not enough woman for a man like you," Esmaa said in a more serious tone.

"You know you have always been my one and only. That hasn't changed. I wanted to marry you but I had promises to keep," Fouad said.

"Since when did they know each other? How long had this been going on?" I asked myself as I watched.

By now, Esmaa was down to her bra and a lacy thong. I couldn't believe my eyes. This could not be happening. I was numb. I wanted to tear myself away from that door but I had to know how Fouad truly felt. Unfortunately, I got more answers than I bargained for and I had many new unanswered questions.

"Well, at least I took advantage of my time in the U.S.," Esmaa asserted. "It was just so tough being without you all those years and then knowing you were in her arms."

"Don't obsess over that nonsense. You know I don't love her. I never have. You are the only woman for me. Fatima was a challenge, a game, a score I had to settle from my past. Now, I finally have her where I want her: at my feet, madly in love," he assured her.

"She's pathetic," Esmaa said. "Does this end in divorce or will I have the pleasure of making her regret she ever met me?"

"Let's not talk about her now. I want to ravish you. Just thinking about being inside you is making me hard. Feel it," he said leading her hand.

"How did I ever live without you? I was crazy to let you go. Now you're mine forever. She'll be dead before I have to share you again. I just put up with it because I knew that in the end, we would have it all. When are you going to tell me the whole story behind your marriage?"

"Patience, my dear. One day I'll tell you the sordid details. For now, the only thing that I can reveal is that the game is not over. I will determine its conclusion in time."

At this point, Fouad had undone her bra and was fondling her breasts.

"Just tell me one thing. Will I have you all to myself soon?" Esmaa said as she turned and started kissing his naked chest.

"In time you will. Remember that I'm already under your spell, my sweet Esmaa. Together, we will do great things; we will conquer the world," Fouad said as he grabbed her by the waist and carried her naked body up to kiss her lips, "Show me how much you love me."

As I quietly exited the house, I could hear the moans from their lovemaking. I had the taxi driver take me back to the hospital. I locked myself in the office and started to sob.

A flood of emotions had invaded my body. I was angry, crushed, devastated, hurt and disgusted. I felt like my soul had been sucked right out of my body. I felt used and humiliated not only by Fouad but also by Esmaa. I squeezed a glass that was on my desk so hard that it shattered in my hand. The pain of the tiny pieces of glass slashing my skin was no comparison to the ache I felt inside.

As I tried to stop the bleeding, I was consumed by my thoughts of Fouad and what he meant by settling a score from the past and everything being a game. I went through the typical motions. First, I wondered if he ever loved me. Something he had clearly indicated otherwise. Then, I speculated what made Esmaa better than me. Finally, I realized it was a moot point. Everything was clear; Fouad had been in love with Esmaa even before we met. He had no respect for our love or for me. I was just a fool who played into his game; an object he used to satisfy his uncontrolled sexual appetite while his heart belonged to someone else.

This answered the question of why Fouad was distant. Looking back, he began to change around the time Esmaa arrived in Antarah. Why marry me if Esmaa was the love of his life? I needed explanations but I couldn't face this situation right now. A mixture of fear and cofussion controlled every fiber of my being. I asked myself was Esmaa truly capable of killing me? Was my life in danger as long as I was married to Fouad?

Luckly, Fouad was leaving the country in two days. He was going on a six- month top secret, no communication, training session. With my husband away, I was not a threat to Esmaa, and I was certain she would be part of the team accompanying him. I was determined not to let on what I had uncovered. The time apart would give me a chance to figure out what to do.

I was suddenly startled by a knock at my door.

"Fatima, can we talk?"

It was just what the doctor ordered, Ibrahim.

"Just a minute," I shouted as I tried to cover my bloody hand with a towel and open the door.

"Are you Ok? Have you been crying? Is your husband all right?" he asked.

"Yes to all your questions," I replied flustered trying to conceal my hand.

"How's the proposal coming along?" he asked.

"It's shaping up nicely," I said.

"Anything you can share?" he asked when suddenly he realized the bloody towel. "Your hand," he said alarmed as he unwrapped the towel without hesitation and quickly grabbed some gauze and alcohol.

At that moment, I just broke down.

"Am I hurting you? How did this happen?" he asked concerned wiping the tears from my cheeks. I looked up and lost myself in his eyes.

"I need some tweezers to remove the glass."

Suddenly, I moved in close and he kissed me. It was just a soft peck on the lips, but I felt a jolt of electricity from head to toe. I wanted to give in to the moment but I wasn't prepared for the consequences of actions taken on the rebound. So, I kept my composure.

"I don't know what I was thinking. Please forgive me," he said. "I need to get my bag and take care of your hand."

"Don't apologize," I said as I put my finger vertically over his lips.

He opened the door and came back to mend my hand. As he removed each sliver of glass I couldn't help thinking about the kiss.

"I'll let you know when the proposal is ready," I stated to distract him from what had just happened.

"By the way, when are we going for the next round of immunizations?" I continued.

"Next week, Insha Allah, God willing."

That afternoon I knew I wasn't ready to face Fouad. I didn't want to stay with Jamila because her husband worked with Fouad and I didn't want to put them in an awkward position. Instead, I asked Dalal if I could crash at her place. Her husband was out of town for a few days and I felt I could trust her because of the bad blood between her and Esmaa. I called Samira and asked her to return to the house to take care of the meals for Fouad. I also asked her to tell Fouad that I had tried to get in touch with him unsuccessfully while at the office. I explained that Dalal wasn't feeling well, her husband was out of town and in her condition I felt she shouldn't be alone. I told her that she didn't have a phone at home, which wasn't uncommon, so just to tell Fouad that I would be spending the night and would see him in the morning.

"Tell him that I love him and I'll miss him tonight," were my last words to Samira.

I had bought myself some time to heal my hand and my heart. I was in pain. That night at Dalal's, I vented. It felt good to talk to someone who knew first hand about Esmaa's cruel intentions. Unfortunately,

Dalal had no answers. She didn't know about Fouad and Esmaa's past relationship yet it didn't surprise her.

"My husband always told me she was not a typical Muslim girl. She was rebellious since childhood. She used to take off for days without a trace. She was the youngest and only girl of seven children. Her father spoiled her rotten. When she decided to go to the U.S. to study, she broke his heart and his wallet. He gave her most of his lifetime savings to fulfill her dream. She never takes "no" for an answer and never enjoys seeing other people happy. I'm very disappointed with Fouad, though. I thought he would see right through her," Dalal said. "Don't shed another tear. They deserve each other. You are too good for that pompous Fouad anyway. Divorce him on the grounds of adultery."

"I wish it were that easy. He's not going to admit to his illicit affairs. With his high rank and connections, he will squirm his way out of it. Most importantly, he is determined to keep me by his side until he carries out his plan. The frightening thing about all of this is that I don't know who this man is and why he hates me so much," I said agitated.

I cried. I cried a lot. I don't know if I ever truly loved Fouad, but, I tried hard to be the woman I thought he wanted me to be. I overlooked his infidelities and worked things out because I felt that we had something special that could grow into love. How could I have been so wrong, so naive? I guess I never had a chance. I felt as empty and frustrated as the evening my father told me I was going to marry a man I didn't know. Why did I think this story would turn out any differently than the way it began? Maybe my father could clear up all my doubts.

The next morning I waited for Fouad to leave the house. It was the day before his trip and I knew he had to head to the base to take care of any loose ends and make sure things would be running smoothly during his absence.

Samira greeted me when I came in. She informed me that Fouad had been out late and wasn't too happy that I had stayed at Dalal's without his permission. I told her to let me know if she heard Fouad's car pull up because I had to make a phone call from the study and I didn't want him to find me there.

I was frantically going through his drawers, file cabinets, anything that would give me answers. I found nothing. Then I called my father. He was in New York at a conference. At least for today, I wouldn't get the information I anxiously needed to uncover Fouad's secrets.

I took a long bath. I scrubbed myself as hard as I had the first time we made love. I felt so dirty and used. After a few hours, I headed to work. When I got there, Fouad was waiting in my office.

"Don't you ever spend the night away from home without my permission," he said as he slapped my face. "You should be grateful that I even let you work. Don't abuse your privileges or I'll have you locked up in the house. You know I'll do it."

"Don't you dare lay a hand on me again," I said as I slapped him back. It felt good to hear that popping sound as I released some of my anger. "What happened to the gentle Fouad that wanted to make our marriage work?" I asked enraged.

He grabbed my arm and noticed my bandaged hand.

"What's this?"

"The reason I didn't go home last night," I said pulling away, "I was in pain, medicated and didn't want to worry you."

"How did it happen?"

"Does it matter?"

"You always know how to push my buttons Fatima," he said grabbing my waist and licking my neck working his way down to my breasts."

"Why does everything with you have to be about sex?"

I tried to push away.

"Don't make me slap you again. You are my wife and I demand respect."

He walked toward the door. I thought he was heading out. Instead, he locked it and came close to me.

"How about if we do it on this desk? I'm leaving tomorrow for six months. You kept me waiting last night. Let's make up for lost time," he said as he put his hand on my thigh.

"Don't touch me," I hissed, removing his hands from my body.

"Are you turning me down?" he said with an agitated voice while sliding his hands up my skirt.

"This is neither the place nor the time," I said as I felt his warm breath on my neck.

I noticed someone was turning the doorknob. When they realized it was locked, they knocked.

"Fatima, are you there?" Dalal asked.

"Fouad let go of me," I said in a low voice.

He straightened up his uniform while I pulled my skirt down in disgust.

"Just a minute," I shouted.

Fouad opened the door and walked out without greeting Dalal. Then, he turned his face towards me.

"I expect to see you at home this afternoon," he said slamming the door.

"Did I interrupt something?" Dalal asked.

"Yes, as a matter of fact, and I'm glad you did. I owe you one."

"I just came to see how you and your hand were doing."

"As well as can be expected. Thank God for work. It's the only thing that will help me keep my sanity. Have you seen Dr. Ibrahim?" I asked.

"He's in surgery for the next hour or so. I know you are going through a rough patch but think things over. Don't make any rash decisions that you might regret. I'm always here for you."

I squeezed her hand.

chapter 16

New Beginnings

I went to Dr. Ibrahim's office right before lunch time and found the door was slightly cracked. When I pushed it open, he was wiping off the sweat from his muscular torso.

"I'm so sorry, I'll come back," I said embarrassed.

"Don't go. Let me put my shirt on," he said. "I just finished doing a couple of miles on the treadmill. I need to release some stress, especially after surgery."

"I didn't know you were a runner," I said as I checked out his tight stomach while his shirt went over his eyes.

Wow! I was surprised at myself. I was reacting like a teenage girl noticing a hot guy for the first time.

"I just brought in the treadmill last week. I've been working long hours so, I thought I could exercise during my down time. May I ask, what brings you by?

"Yes, you may. A lunch invitation."

"What's the special occasion?" Dr. Ibrahim asked.

"Our future endeavors."

"I'd be delighted to have lunch with you," he said. "Do you like falafel? I know the best falafel shop in town."

"Sounds great."

"Just give me a little time to wash up, do salat, prayer, and change. I'll meet you at your office."

Ibrahim and I had a nice lunch. We talked about our project and scheduling our meeting for the upcoming week when I knew Fouad would be gone. After lunch, it was back to the office for a couple of hours and then home. Fouad wasn't there which was good because I was faking being ill to avoid any physical contact. He came home rather late and seemed very tired. Probably Esmaa had worn him out.

"How was your day?" I asked.

"Very busy," he replied. "What's wrong with you?"

"I've been sick since this afternoon. Maybe something I ate."

"So, are you going to make our last night memorable?" he asked.

"I'll be right back, Fouad," I rushed to the bathroom and stayed in for a while.

"Are you Ok?" he asked after knocking on the bathroom door.

"I'll be right out."

When I came out, he was lying in bed.

"Come next to me. Are you feeling any better?" he asked.

As I walked toward the bed, images of Fouad and Esmaa flashed through my mind. I wanted to react irrationally based on my memories but fought hard not to give in to my emotions. In bed, he hugged my body against his.

"Let me just feel you," he said.

"I'm sorry about tonight," I said in a sad voice wanting him to believe I had regrets for the lack of intimacy.

"It's all right," he said as he dozed off.

The next morning he was up before the sun. Samira had packed all his things and put them in his study.

"Do you have everything?" I asked.

"Just about. I won't be calling you for a long time. I will be out in the field working on some very delicate operations, so I'll have to focus all my attention on what I'm doing. There will be no contact number, no exact location. If there's an emergency, I want you to call Rauf. If he can't help, he'll know where to reach me. I'll miss you so much but I know Samira will take good care of you," he said hugging me tight.

"I'll look after Fatima. Don't worry about a thing," Samira replied.

"Everything will be fine, Fouad," I insisted.

Samira wished Fouad well and left us alone.

"Come here, Fatima. Kiss me goodbye," he demanded.

I gave him a quick peck on the lips.

"What's wrong with you?" he asked as he grabbed me forcefully.

"You're hurting me," I paused. "I guess I'm a little upset. Your job is so demanding. You think I enjoy watching you leave for months at a time? Not being able to contact you? Not even knowing where you are or even if you are alive?"

"You know what my job entails," he said.

"I thought it would get easier with time but it just gets more difficult," I said with tears in my eyes. It was quite a performance if I say so myself. I gave him a big hug. "Be safe."

"Thanks sweetheart," he responded followed by a kiss that I couldn't refuse.

As he walked away, I wiped my mouth in disgust. He was finally gone and I wished he would never come back. All the hurt, the anger, the disillusionment, it all left with him. I felt relieved, free. Focusing my attention on my work at the hospital would be the best therapy. Making a difference and getting back a sense of self that had been diminished by Fouad's repeated betrayals was important to my sanity.

I had a big breakfast and headed to work full of energy and excitement. I was my old self again, if only for some months. I called the Presidential Palace and set up the appointment for our presentation.

I called Dr. Ibrahim and gave him the good news. In a couple of days, we would be meeting with the president and hopefully gaining his support to move along with our project.

It was great coming home and not having to worry about Fouad and his demands. Spending hours watching American movies, listening to Frank Sinatra tapes, everything that got on Fouad's nerves, was delightful. It felt good to bring back the memories of my life in Washington D.C. and my college days in Boston. I even called some of my school buddies to reminisce about the good times. I avoided talking about my life and what it had become and focused on the positives, my work at the hospital and my future plans.

The next day, I was able to talk to Baba. At first, he tried to avoid giving me any explanations.

"I will have a serious talk with Fouad when he gets back," he said.

"No. I don't want him involved, I just need answers. Why did you arrange my marriage to Fouad? Why him? He mentioned something about settling an old score. What's going on? What don't I know?"

"This is a delicate conversation that I will only have face to face," Baba said.

"That's fine. I will go see you in Washington if that's what it takes."

"Fatme, not now. Give me some time to straighten out some Embassy business and I promise I'll go to Antarah and tell you everything."

"Okay, Baba. Just don't keep me waiting for long. I love you, and nothing you could tell me will make me love you less. Trust me."

I was somewhat relieved that in a matter of days I would have answers but not soon enough. That evening I barely slept imagining what secrets my father would bring to light, yet trying to keep myself focused for our morning meeting with the president.

I wore the most fabulous suit I had in my closet. It was something I had brought from the U.S. and managed to salvage from Fouad's destructive hands. It was a black, fitted, 3 button blazer with a matching skirt which I put together with an off white, silky, collarless blouse, a pearl necklace and earrings, a pair of sheer black hose and some very high, black pumps. A black scarf covered my hair and on my lapel, a golden, camel broach that my father had given to me as a gift. I was dressed to kill.

I gathered all the paperwork, placed it in my briefcase and headed to the palace to meet Dr. Ibrahim. When I arrived, he was waiting for me. He was wearing an Italian tailored, double-breasted, navy blue suit with a bright white shirt and a white and navy striped tie. He looked so handsome.

"You are a vision in black," he said.

"You look quite handsome yourself," I replied.

We went through a metal detector as we headed towards the president's office. When we entered, President Saeed was sitting at his desk.

"Good morning, Mr. President," I said.

"Good morning, my lovely Fatima," he said as he stood up to shake my hand.

"This is Dr. Ibrahim Al-Kateb," I said as they shook hands.

"It's an honor, Mr. President," Dr. Ibrahim said.

"My son speaks highly of you and your work at the hospital. Sit down. Rauf tells me you recently came from America. Many of our young men get their student visas to America and other parts of the world promising to come back to work and share their knowledge and don't return. You are the exception. I'm proud of you," the president expressed.

The meeting was off to a great start.

"So, Fatima, Dr. Al-Kateb, tell me about this idea to improve our health system."

"Well, it was mostly Mrs. Aziz's idea…" Dr. Ibrahim said.

We were with the president for over an hour. The meeting was a success. The president was very impressed with our proposal. He gave us the go ahead to start organizing the fundraiser and he committed government funds to jump-start the project.

"So, where are we going to celebrate our victory?" Dr. Ibrahim asked.

"You name the place," I said.

"Are you up for a drive? I know this wonderful seafood restaurant overlooking the Mediterranean. It's about 30 minutes away from here."

"Let's go. We could discuss the fundraiser on our way there."

Lunch was great. We ate a fish that is native to the area and is coincidently called Sultan Brahim, short for Ibrahim. This is a small fish that has a neon yellow stripe running across the top of its body. What makes this fish special is that its bones are soft and edible. We ate a generous portion of fried fish, fried potatoes, salad and hummus with pita bread.

"Dr. Ibrahim …" I said.

"Please, call me Brahim, especially if we are not in the hospital."

"Brahim, thanks for this lovely lunch. This place is breathtaking. The perfect place to kick off our future plans."

"I'm glad to see you smiling again," he said. "I hate to pry but why are you so sad most of the time?"

"I appreciate your concern but I rather not talk about it. I don't want to spoil a perfect day."

"I'm your friend. You can trust me," he said.

"I'm in a loveless marriage and my husband is cheating on me," I blurted out.

"I'm sorry to hear that."

"I wish my life were different. I wish I was in D.C. living my old life; a life where things weren't so complicated."

"I truly wish you were happy."

"I know you do. Thanks."

"Look at the bright side; we would have never met if you were in D.C."

"You're right," I responded with a slight smile on my face.

On the ride back, I was quiet. I wished Ibrahim were Fouad. I wished we had met in the U.S., fallen madly in love, married and never looked back. I wished we could run off together and disappear where no one could find us. But, I couldn't do that to Ibrahim. He had a life devoted to medicine. He was single, unattached and available with dreams, I'm sure, to remarry and build his future. I couldn't be part of it. It was morally and legally impossible.

The following day, I found a dozen red roses on my desk with a note.

"Congratulations on a successful meeting."

There was no signature, but I knew they were from Brahim. He was the only one who could always put a smile on my face.

For the next week, we worked closely putting the final touches to our anticipated event. We kept it professional, never mentioning our heart to heart conversation. I kept referring to him as Dr. Ibrahim.

Baba had agreed to come for the fundraiser. I hoped that whatever he had to say might give me an out to my situation with Fouad. Maybe I would have solid grounds for a divorce and could dream of a future with Brahim.

The fundraiser was going to take place in the same theater where we met for the first time; a place of bittersweet memories. We had booked the finest musical acts in Antarah and even some musical guests from neighboring Arabic countries. We had already received more than a few, hefty donations that had allowed us to purchase three of the ten vans needed for our project. Professionally, things were very good.

The day of the event was finally here. Nabil, Jamila's husband, had volunteered to go with little Ramee to pick Baba up from the airport and bring him home. I was swamped with last minute details and couldn't pull away. I knew he would enjoy spending time with Ramee, the closest he had to a grandson. I came home just in time to kiss Baba hello and get ready for the evening.

One of Antarah's best seamstresses had sewn a dress that I had designed. It was a satin black, strapless long dress with a full, long skirt and intricate embroidery on the chest and on the hem line. The scarf made to match the dress wrapped around my hair and then fell as a shawl covering my exposed shoulders. I wore a diamond solitaire necklace with matching earrings.

I was so excited to be escorted by Baba. He wore his tuxedo and was so proud of me.

"My gorgeous Fatme, you're just like me. When you put your mind to it, the sky's the limit."

"I learned from the best," I said hugging him and kissing his forehead.

When we arrived to the theater, it was crowded. There was a line of limos unloading the most prominent people in the country. Security was tight, the whole presidential family and all of the government officials were there. I looked for Brahim but couldn't find him.

My father was stopped constantly on our way in. Too many people were greeting us and congratulating us for the evening's successful turn out. Some people asked about Fouad, someone I would rather not think about on this special day. Fouad was synonymous with my failures not my achievements. Today, I celebrated the woman I had always wanted and knew I could be, not the Fatima that was reduced to being a victim of a malicious plot.

As we walked into the theater, I spotted a very pregnant Dalal and her husband and introduced them to Baba. We also met up with Jamila and Nabil, Nur and some other close friends. Then, at a distance, I saw him, Dr. Ibrahim. He walked toward us.

"Father, I want you to meet Dr. Ibrahim Al-Kateb, my partner in crime. This event is also his success."

"Dr. Al-Kateb, it is a pleasure to meet you. Both of you make a good team."

"The pleasure is all mine, Mr. Ambassador. Your daughter speaks highly of you."

Dr. Ibrahim was staring at me.

"Are you and your wife going to be sitting with us?" Baba asked.

"Just me, Sir," he replied.

"Fatme go ahead with Dr. Al-Kateb while I go greet President Saeed and his family."

"You look stunning," Dr. Ibrahim said.

"Thank you, even though your stares are making me a little nervous," I replied.

"You just look more beautiful than the day I met you in this theater for the first time if that is even possible," Dr. Ibrahim said.

"You are making me blush."

As we walked towards our seats, we saw Rauf.

"You get prettier every time I see you."

"Rauf, how are you?" I asked.

"Not as fine as you," he replied moving in close and whispering.

"Dr. Al-Kateb, congratulations to both of you on this spectacular evening," as he shook Brahim's hand.

"Thank you Rauf."

"By the way, I kept your husband informed of your project. He deeply regrets not being here or calling you but he sent you this," Rauf said as he handed me an envelope. "Aren't you going to open it?"

"The show is about to start. I'll see you during intermission," I said.

I walked away with Dr. Ibrahim and started crumbling the envelope.

"Are you sure you want to do that?" Dr. Ibrahim asked as I threw it in a nearby trash can.

"Nothing is going to spoil this evening."

When we got to our seats, my father and our closest friends including Samira were all there. The night was magical. We had been able to raise more money than anticipated which meant that our ideas were going to become realities. The poor and the children of Antarah would have access to health care even in remote regions. I think I smiled all night.

As we said our goodbyes, Baba collapsed. Dr. Ibrahim immediately loosened Baba's bow tie and unbuttoned his shirt. When he realized he had no pulse and wasn't breathing, he performed C.P.R. while others called for an ambulance. I was numb. Dr. Ibrahim worked hard on Baba trying to revive him but nothing could be done. I saw the disappointment in his eyes.

In a matter of minutes, my blissfulness turned to agony. I dropped to the ground and grabbed on to his lifeless body hugging it tight. I never wanted to let go. It took several men, including Brahim, to pull me off his body. I was in shock. It was too much to absorb at once. A piece of me had died. Again, the theater became a bittersweet stage for a devastating episode of my life.

The people around me tried to console me but the echo of their voices pounded in my head. In my confusion, I took a cab and rushed home. I wanted to cry but I was consumed with rage. I kept reliving the memory of the day Baba told me I was to marry Fouad. I remembered my wedding night, the way Fouad raped me again and again. It was Baba who offered me as a sacrificial lamb. All my love had turned to hate.

Suddenly, I came face to face with my precious camel collection. Those were the mementos that captured my relationship with Baba. With one forceful swipe, I watched each figurine fall and break into tiny pieces just like Baba had broken my heart when he handed me over to that monster I called a husband.

Would I ever forgive Baba for what my life had become especially now that he had taken my hopes, my dreams and my answers to the grave?

The ring from the phone snapped me out of it. It was Nabil who felt the urgency to share his last conversation with Baba. I really didn't want to talk but I didn't want to hurt Jamila by hanging up on her husband, so I listened.

"I'm so sorry for your loss. Your father had been in New York running some tests on his heart. The doctors had told him he needed open- heart surgery and he chose to postpone the operation until after his trip. He was afraid to die without seeing you one more time. I thought you'd want to know."

I was emotionless even though I knew that my inquiries about Fouad had forced Baba to come to Antarah and neglect his health.

Maybe I was to blame but I was blinded by hate.

The next morning, Fouad called to offer his sympathy. I guess this constituted a real emergency. I told Samira to take a message, to tell him I took some sleeping pills or something. He said he'd be back for the funeral that evening.

With no sleep and no desire to be social, I put on a black dress and scarf to tend to a house full of people, mostly strangers, offering their condolences.

Everyone was very concerned about me particularly Jamila, who loved Baba as her own. She probably thought she was the only one who could understand my loss oblivious to the fact that I was responsible for his death and felt no remorse about it.

Throughout the day, I received several telegrams and phone calls from Washington D.C. including a call from the President of the United States who was a close friend.

As the men were ready to head to the cemetery, Fouad arrived.

"My dearest Fatima, I'm so sorry about your father. He was a good man. My father always held him with great regards. It's truly a terrible loss," he said.

"Thanks for coming. I know you are breaking military protocol just to be by my side," I said.

"I know how hard it is to lose a father. I lost both my parents within a short period of time," he said as his eyes watered. This was probably the only sincere statement that had come out of his mouth since we met.

For a few seconds, I actually felt sorry for him until my heart started holding him responsible for what had happened.

I was relieved that I did not have to go with them. Baba was going to be buried next to Mama and they would be together again. I wondered how many of his secrets she had taken to the grave or was she a victim like me.

Right before they left to the cemetery, Dr. Ibrahim came to pay his respects. His presence meant a lot. I yearned for him to hold me and tell me that everything would be all right. Instead, Fouad kissed me goodbye.

"Don't forget, if you need anything call Rauf," he insisted.

Right after the body was laid to rest, Fouad was gone.

The crowd came back to the house where Samira had prepared food and coffee for everyone. People praised Baba's accomplishments and remembered his relationship with Mama and how much they longed for a child. Through it all, I sat calmly listening. Even President Saeed told us some stories about Baba that put a smile on everybody's face but mine. At this point, I just wanted everyone to leave and be alone.

I was exhausted. So, I excused myself and went to my room. As I undressed, I realized there was a camel figurine on my dresser with a note.

"Dear Fatme:

I had a local D.C. artist make this camel just for you. I thought it would be a nice addition to your collection. Always follow your heart because Mama and I will be there to guide you. Love, Baba"

This was the first time that I yelled.

"Why?" I cried inconsolably. "Why did you take the only person I had left in this world?" I looked up defying God.

I cried for days and even though Jamila and Samira tried to comfort me, for several weeks my life was consumed by guilt and regrets. I was so depressed that I hardly ate and mostly slept all day.

Jamila brought little Ramee over on a daily basis to cheer me up while Dalal kept me informed on Dr. Ibrahim's progress with our project. She encouraged me to return to work because I was missed and needed at the hospital, but nothing lifted my spirits.

"Dr. Ibrahim keeps asking about you. He is concerned. I think he misses his working partner. He is under a lot of pressure trying to get the project off the ground, keeping up with his patient load and performing surgeries at the hospital. He needs you. You can't throw away all your hard work. You have to keep your dreams alive. That's what your father would have wanted," Dalal said.

"I appreciate your words. I just don't know how to keep living. Baba was the only one who could unmask Fouad. Now, I don't know what I'm up against. Baba was my lifeline. Now, he's gone. I'm all alone," I said.

"That's not true. You have your friends; you have Jamila and me, who are like your sisters. You have Dr. Ibrahim…" she insisted.

"Dr. Ibrahim is an impossibility. My only hope of happily ever after disappeared with Baba. He took his secrets to the grave and now I may never know who Fouad really is."

"You have to focus on your commitment to the people of Antarah. Remember the poor, the children, the sick; remember how Allah blessed you with the knowledge and the contacts to make a difference. You have to fight the fight and ask God to guide your future. Allah never abandons us."

"Are you sure about that? I feel deserted by Allah."

"Allah is always with you and He will give you the strength to get out of bed and start rebuilding your life. Just have faith, Fatima."

"It's not that simple. I'm not good for anyone right now. I need more time to sort out my life. I need more time to mourn my loss; to feel sorry for myself. I'm so tired. I'm not giving up; I'm just not there yet," I said holding back the tears and giving her a hug. "Take care of yourself and thank you for being a good friend."

"He asks about you," Dalal whispered in my ear as she hugged me back.

chapter **17**

The Love Affair

I woke up determined to start living again and seek answers to all the questions that kept haunting me. I headed to work. I felt guilty that I had abandoned Brahim and our projects.

As I settled into my office, the door behind me closed.

"Welcome back," Dr. Ibrahim said as he hugged me tight. "I really missed you."

"I'm so sorry," I tried to blurt out as he caressed my lips with his.

I didn't know what had gotten into him and I didn't care. The kiss was magical, like a dream, an out of body experience. I felt as if I had never been kissed until that moment. Five minutes, ten minutes, I lost track of time. It was so breathtaking that I could have stayed in that moment forever.

"Wow! Don't stop," I said.

"It's too risky," Dr. Ibrahim replied.

"Do you regret what just happened?"

"Of course not. I've wanted to kiss you since the first time I saw you. I've replayed this moment in my mind thousands of times. I just didn't anticipate that it would exceed my expectations," he said giving me that charming smile.

"Come here," I said extending my arms. "Just hold me a little longer. I missed you so much. I just couldn't bare the thought of seeing you and not being able to express myself like I just did. I also owe you an apology because I never thanked you for everything you tried to do to save my father. I truly appreciated your efforts."

"I would have done anything to spare you that pain."

"I know that."

"I thought I might not see you again. I asked Dalal about you, discretely of course."

"She told me. I just needed time. Thanks for giving it to me."

"So, are you ready for some good news?" Dr. Ibrahim asked.

"Always," I replied.

"The fundraiser was a tremendous success. We were able to purchase all ten vans. I've already signed leases for seven clinic locations and this week I received the government funds to start equipping them. I've also gotten firm commitments from my colleagues to volunteer. Everything is going as planned," he said.

"You are truly amazing," I said.

"Thanks," he paused. "Is Fouad still out of town?"

"Are you sure you want to." I attempted to ask until he put his finger over my lips.

"The question is are you sure?"

"Why don't we go to that quaint restaurant where we had lunch last time and talk about this a little more?"

"I think it's an excellent idea. I'll clear my schedule for the rest of the afternoon."

On the way to the restaurant, we held hands in the car and gazed into each others eyes every opportunity we had. I felt like I was going on my first date. I was so scared yet so excited. When we got to the restaurant, we asked to be seated where we could have some privacy.

"Brahim,"

"I love when you say my name," he interrupted.

"We are really taking a big risk. I'm a married woman. I don't know if I will ever be able to get a divorce. You are young, handsome, a doctor, why me? You could have any woman you want. I see the way all the single women at the hospital look at you. You can do so much better than me; someone uncomplicated who can devote herself to making you happy. I just can't do that. Not because I don't want to, but because I can't."

"I don't want any other woman. I want you. I never thought I could ever feel this way about anyone after my wife's passing but then you came along and you changed my life," he asserted.

"Are you willing to die for this love? Because you know that if anyone finds out about us, Fouad will kill both of us."

"I was dead before I met you. I was going through the motions. I love my job but it isn't enough. When we met, you brought the spark back; you gave me a reason to wake up every morning."

"You did the same for me. I tried to keep my marriage together but after so many betrayals, I gave up. I felt like dying and the thought of you kept me alive."

I could hear a bit of commotion in the background as if someone important had arrived.

"What a surprise!" Rauf said walking towards our table. "I'm so glad to see you Fatima, Dr. Ibrahim."

"Rauf, what a pleasant coincidence," I said. "Today was my first day back at work, so Dr. Al-Kateb brought me to lunch to share all the progress he's made with our project."

"I've heard things are going great with that," Rauf replied.

"Yes, everything is running smoothly, especially now that Mrs. Aziz is back with us," Dr. Ibrahim said. "How's the president doing?"

"He's great, thanks for asking," Rauf replied. "I spoke to Fouad yesterday. He's doing well. I'll have to tell him that you are looking well and that you're back to work. Have you spoken to him lately?"

"No. He told me not to expect any phone calls for a while just an occasional letter. When you speak to him, tell him that I miss him and can't wait for him to come home," I said.

"Well, it was a pleasure but I have to run. My group is waiting," Rauf said.

"Take care Rauf, send our regards to your father," I said. After he left I continued. "This is exactly the kind of thing I'm talking about. We have to be extremely careful. You never know who can be watching."

"We'll be careful."

When we got back to the hospital, we found out Dalal had given birth to a little girl, Sarah. Both mother and daughter were doing fine. Her husband was by her side full of excitement. My dreams of motherhood had started to fade.

After a few weeks of long working hours, our project was finally up and running. Brahim was long overdue for a vacation and invited me to go with him for a week. This was a big step and I wasn't sure if I was ready. My brain gave me all the reasons why I shouldn't go through with it but my heart wanted to discover the meaning of true love. I gave instructions to Samira on how to handle anyone calling for me including the remote possibility of a call from Fouad. I also covered my bases with Jamila, Dalal, and a few other close friends. I told all of them that I needed to go to Washington to put all of my father's affairs in order; that I needed some time away in a different environment.

I contacted my father's attorney in Washington D.C. and told him I would rather lease than sell our home. I couldn't part with my childhood memories. I also told him that if anyone called asking about me this week, he was to tell them that I was tied up in meetings pertaining to my father's businesses. He was to contact me on my cell phone, a number that only Samira and he knew, if anyone inquired about me.

Although my father's lawyer was taking care of most of my father's last wishes, I was planning a trip to D.C. the week after embarking on my dangerous adventure.

I went on a modest shopping spree and bought a bathing suit and a few revealing articles of clothing. I saw a beautiful belly-dancing outfit and I remembered my mom. I thought it would be fun to try it on. I loved the way it looked on me, so I bought it. I also purchased a black, strict Muslim garment that covered all of my body and a khimar, which is similar to a scarf to conceal my entire head. It had a built-in thin net over my eyes to allow me to see and breathe. This was the safest way to disguise my identity.

I didn't know where we were going but it was almost summertime and very warm. I packed light; just the bare essentials and the few extra things I had shopped for. I had our chauffeur drive me to the airport. I then entered a restroom, changed into my black garment and waited for Brahim. When I saw him, I walked up and told him to walk towards the car and I would follow. I was terrified yet exhilarated by it. I kept my face covered until we left the city. But I kept a scarf over my head, just in case I was forced to cover my face quickly. Brahim then pulled over on the side of the road and started kissing me.

"I feel I'm in a dream."

"It's not a dream. This is real," he said kissing me again.

"So, where are we going?"

"We are going to my chalet on the beach. It's my favorite place in the whole world. I bought it when I returned to Antarah. It was the property I always wanted to own here. It's modest, probably not like the places you are used to, but it's my retreat; where I go to think, to meditate, to dream. It's a two-hour drive and its location is somewhat isolated. It would be far enough so that no one would recognize you."

"It sounds perfect. I'm just ecstatic you would want to share it with me," I said squeezing his hand. "Brahim, tell me everything about you."

"I come from a very tight knit family. Both my mother and father are alive and have a very close relationship. I have six brothers and three sisters. I'm the middle child. I'm the only one who left Antarah and now I'm back."

"Why did you leave Antarah?"

"I wanted more. I had a dream of becoming a doctor. I don't know if you are familiar with our educational system but here, the government assigns you a major to study in college based on your high school grade point average. I was five points below what I needed to study medicine. Instead, the government had chosen engineering as my future career. Frustrated, I headed to the U.S. Embassy in hopes of getting a visa. I guess it was meant to be because two months later, on my 19th birthday, I arrived in the land of opportunity."

"What a great story. I'm sure your family was so happy for you but at the same time saddened by your decision to leave."

"It wasn't easy on any of us but I felt I could give them a better life if I pursued my goals in the States"

"Tell me more."

"Are you sure I'm not boring you?"

"Never," I said kissing his hand.

"I started at a small community college studying English as a second language. I had studied English here but I knew there was much more to learn if I wanted to be accepted into Boston University."

"Oh my God! I went to Smith College in Northampton. I can't believe we were less than two hours away. One weekend a month, my friends and I used to hang out in Boston. Who knows how many times our paths crossed?"

"That's truly incredible. I guess it really is a small world. Smith, isn't that an all girl college?"

"Only the best for a strict Muslim girl. So, what happened next?"

"I got accepted to B.U. with a full scholarship. After three years, I applied to their Medical School and got accepted. It's not the norm but I fulfilled all of their requirements. Another six years, including my fellowship, and I was a bona fide doctor. During and after my two year fellowship, I worked at the Franciscan Children's Hospital," he said modestly.

"Wow! Why pediatric surgery?"

"I love children and I love challenges."

"So, was I a challenge?"

"No, you were the impossible. I still can't believe that this is happening."

At this point we had already been driving for about an hour and we made a quick stop to get something to drink. Before we got out of the car, we kissed several times. We couldn't stop staring at each other. We couldn't believe we were together at last. We got some drinks and snacks and kept going.

"Now, it's your turn," he said.

"What do you mean?" I asked.

"Tell me about you."

"I was raised in Washington D.C., I lived a very privileged life; went to an all-girls school and college. Wanted to pursue a Master's in social work and got my dreams cut short because of my marriage. That's my life in a nutshell."

"May I ask, why Fouad?"

"It was an arranged marriage. Believe me no one was more surprised and disappointed than I was. It had barely been a year since my mother died and I had come home for Eid. My father received a phone call and, next thing I knew, he was telling me that after graduation, I was getting married. An arranged marriage was totally ludicrous to me. My father knew how I felt. I wasn't brought up under the assumption that I was going to marry a man that had already been hand picked for me."

"So, how did it happen?"

"I don't know the details. I just remember he was on the phone and sounded very agitated. I loved and respected my father too much to challenge what he had decided for me. On this last visit to Antarah, I hoped to learn the real reason for my union with Fouad. He was going to tell me but never got the chance," I said breaking down.

"Don't cry, Fatima. I hate to see you sad."

"I need to talk about it. I just could never understand how this happened. I never liked the military life. I admired my father and his accomplishments but I remember listening to Mama gripe about how lonely she felt when he was in the military and how demanding he was as a result of his environment. Fortunately,

I came along when he was already an Ambassador and had an extravagant life. That's probably when my mother and father started enjoying their marriage. It was more about socializing and entertaining. My mother thrived in the limelight."

"Tell me about her."

"Her name was Iman; she was a wonderful mother and a kind, beautiful human being. She died, way too soon, of cancer. She kept her illness from me till her last days. I was very hurt because I felt I was robbed of quality time we could have spent together if I had only known. My father and I were very close but it just wasn't the same without her, especially when the issue of my marriage came along. I feel my mother wouldn't have allowed it. She would have fought my father on it. I just couldn't do it. He had already lost my mother and I felt it wasn't right for me to question his motives. I knew he loved me with all his heart so I believed he would not allow anything bad to happen to his little girl. I truly think he didn't know what Fouad was capable of."

"So, how bad is it?"

"It's worse than bad. Since day one, he cheated on me. At first, I felt responsible because I made it obvious that I detested him. With time, I took my friends' advice and put my all to making it work. There was a time when I really thought we were on track. Then, I walked in on him with another woman. It was the day you and I met."

"That explains why you left early that night."

"Yes. After that, I just went through the motions but I knew it wasn't going to be happily ever after. When he got shot, I put my life in perspective. I was willing to forgive and forget. Maybe life was giving us a second chance. Then, I came home early one day and found him with one of his co-workers, a woman I considered a friend. They were laughing and ridiculing me. From what I gathered, this woman was the love of his life and I was just a pawn in his schemes."

"Did you confront them?"

"No. I wanted to find out the truth from my father first so I could tackle the situation in an intelligent manner. But, that day never came. I'm clueless, angry…"

Suddenly, Brahim stopped the car.

"Be honest with me. Do you love him?"

"No. Maybe I did once. I don't even know. I just know that he used me and for that I despise him." I paused. "Now you know everything. You can still back out of this. I wouldn't hold it against you. My life is a mess. I might be involved in a dangerous scheme. I don't know what my future holds," I said afraid of being rejected.

"Whatever the future holds, we'll face it together. I won't abandon you. We've come this far and I'm not turning back," he said as he caressed my face and wiped my tears.

"Brahim." I started to say as he put his finger over my lips and then got closer and kissed me.

chapter 18

Our Mediterranean Sunsets

We arrived at the chalet. It was right on the beach, but I wasn't familiar with this area, since it wasn't a "touristy" spot. It was fantastic. Most of the surrounding chalets were vacant because it was too early in the summer. I felt relieved, relaxed, and at peace.

When Brahim opened the door, I could smell fresh flowers.

"How do you like my home?" he asked.

As I looked around, I saw all these beautiful flowers, fresh fruit, colored, candied almonds. Then, I looked out the glass double doors and saw the most breathtaking Mediterranean sunset.

"I love it. When did you do all of this?" I asked.

"I can't take all the credit. My mother prepared everything to my specifications."

"Does she know about us?"

"She knows there is someone," he said. "I want you to meet her soon."

"I'd love that."

"Isn't that the most beautiful sunset you've ever seen?" he asked.

"Everything about this place is enchanting."

"I'm happy you are pleased."

"Anyplace would make me happy as long as I'm with you."

"Come on," he said taking me by the hand.

We took our shoes off and ran towards the shore. As the chilly water tickled our feet, we kissed passionately while the sun went down and disappeared in the horizon.

"Everyday, at this same time, we will stand right here and the Mediterranean sunset will witness every chapter of our love story," he said.

"I never imagined you would be such a romantic."

"There's still a lot about me you don't know but in time you'll know everything. Let's go in. Would you like to pray by my side?"

"Yes."

When we returned to the chalet, we did wudu. This ritual is obligatory before engaging in prayer. A person must wash their hands three times, rinse their mouth three times, and then splash water into their nose, forehead, ears, face, arms, and feet. This process has to be repeated three times.

As I came out of the bathroom, Brahim was laying the two msalaeeh on the floor. This moment of reflection had brought me great inner peace.

I got up and left Brahim deep in thought.

"Allah, how could something so wrong feel so right? I know I'm going against Your teachings. I know that I'm committing a sin. Yet, all I could do is ask for Your forgiveness and guidance. I just love her too much and I feel You have brought her into my life so I can protect her and make her happy. Please, show me the way."

When I saw Brahim putting the rugs away, I walked up to him and gave him a big hug. We stayed like that for a few minutes.

"Are you hungry habeebtee?" he asked.

"A little ayunnee, my eyes."

Everything felt so right, so natural. After a light dinner on the deck overlooking the water, we went for a walk on the beach. We held hands as if we never wanted to let go.

"Habeebtee Fatme, I want you to know there is no pressure. We don't have to rush anything. We will go at your pace. I don't want you to regret any moment with me. I want you to be ready and to take every step knowing it is what you want."

I rubbed his hands then kissed them softly. "I'm actually a little tired."

We went back in.

"This will be your room. It has a bathroom. I also took the liberty of getting you a few things," he said.

"An oversized Boston University t-shirt. How'd you know? I love to sleep in t-shirts."

"I brought it with me from the states. I guess all this time I was saving it for you. I also got you some scented candles, some rose petals for your bath, slippers and this robe. I want you to relax and pamper yourself. Forget about the world and enjoy our time together."

I kissed him on the forehead.

Then, he took me by the hand.

"This is my room. You are welcome anytime. This house is your house. Feel free to open the fridge, drink, eat, make yourself at home."

"Thank you. Are you going to sleep?"

"I'm going to shower and then I'll read a little from the Qur'an," he said.

"I'll come say good night."

"I'll be waiting."

I took a nice bubble bath with rose petals. I put on my oversized t-shirt with my favorite boxer shorts that I had brought from the house and wrapped myself in the robe. I also covered my hair before I walked to his room.

"What do you think?"

"May I?" he said as he got closer, ready to undo my hijab.

"I need more time," I said taking a few steps back even though I wanted to throw myself in his arms.

Even though I was totally against the hijab when I first arrived to Antarah because I felt it was Fouad's way of controlling me, I had learned to understand that the hijab empowered women. It was a symbol of self-respect and honor and I actually felt naked and vulnerable if I took it off in front of someone who wasn't my husband. Granted, I was ready to break all the rules but revealing my hair was only going to happen when I decided to give myself body and soul to Brahim.

"Maybe it's dumb, but I want you to see my hair when the time is right."

"So, I guess this is good night."

"Come here," he said. "No good night kiss?"

I went up to him and gave him a soft kiss on the lips.

"Sweet dreams habeebtee," he said

"Tesbah al kher, good night, ayunnee." I went to my bedroom. I fought hard to overcome my carnal desires but I didn't want to rush into anything; it needed to be right. Tomorrow was another day. I also fought my thoughts of guilt and wondered if I was making the biggest mistake of my life. Not because of Brahim, but because of the consequences if Fouad ever found out.

I woke up early. I barely slept. I kept thinking about Brahim and wondering if he felt the same way I did. I suspected he did and admired his self-control.

"Good morning," I said giving him a kiss.

"It's a great morning now."

"Why is that?"

"Because I have the most incredible woman I've ever known by my side," he said as he held me tight.

"Flattery won't get you anywhere. Did you sleep well?"

"Did you?"

"I asked first."

"If you're asking, did I have a desperate need to feel your body next to mine all night last night? Yes I did."

"Well, I slept like a baby. That mattress is excellent," I said.

"I'm glad habeebtee," he said as he rubbed my shoulders.

"So, what's on the agenda today?"

"Anything you want as long as we're back on time to be at our special place before sun down."

"I wouldn't miss that date for anything in the world." I suddenly glanced at his entertainment center.

"Sinatra tapes," I said excited.

"My favorite singer."

"I can't believe it, mine too. I met "old blue eyes" at a White House function once."

"No way. Was he nice?"

"I was very young. But, I guess. He signed my tape and kissed me on the cheek. I remember his piercing blue eyes; they lit up a room. Even as a child, I knew there was something special about him. As I grew older and listened to his music, I fell in love with his songs. What's your favorite?"

"Fly Me to the Moon," he said.

"Mine too," I said.

He walked up to his tape collection, put a tape in the stereo system and fast forwarded it to a song. "Fly me to the moon let me play among the stars, let me know what love is like on Jupiter and Mars…."

As I listened, he took me by the hand and we started dancing to our favorite Sinatra tune. It was like a dream. He was a good dancer. We probably danced for half an hour until the first side of the tape finished. One romance song after the other, we held each other and kissed while our bodies moved to the music.

"Isn't it amazing how we have so much in common," he said.

"It really is. Thanks for helping me make such beautiful memories. And by the way, you are a great dancer."

"You too," he said. "Let's go have some lunch and afterwards we can go to the market to buy some fresh meat and vegetables to grill tonight."

"Sounds like a plan."

While we were out in public, I restrained from gestures of affection. I also was prepared to cover my face at a second's notice if anyone looked familiar. It was hard to hide like this. It was also wrong. I asked God for forgiveness and hoped he would have mercy on my soul. I was trapped from the beginning, I didn't plan this but, I guess maktub, it was written; it was part of my destiny and I was going to live this moment like I had never lived before. After lunch and the market, we headed back to the chalet.

When the sun started to set, we went to the shore and, again, kissed passionately until the sun disappeared.

"Every time I see a Mediterranean sunset, I'll think of you," he said.

"And I'll think of you, and of this moment and every moment we share after this one."

We went back, washed and prayed. Many people would think our prayers were pointless but it is the duty of a Muslim to pray five times a day; at sunrise, noon, after four o'clock, at sunset and an hour and a half after the sunset prayer.

I was slowly catching on to this routine. It was unfortunate that my parents didn't instill this habit in me as a child. I guess it wasn't too late to start now.

Afterwards, I helped Brahim in the kitchen.

"A doctor and a chef… I'm impressed," I said.

"And, the best is yet to come…" he said humming a Sinatra tune.

We were good together. Even in the kitchen, we complimented each other. He was so funny and talkative. He put an eternal smile on my face.

After dinner, I cleaned up and then we went for a walk. When we came back, we sat for a few minutes.

"I'll be out shortly, I'm going to take a shower," I said.

"I'm not going anywhere."

I took a nice long shower. I came out in my robe.

"You look refreshed and radiant," he said.

"Thanks."

There was soft, instrumental Arabic music playing. The lights were dim and scented candles were burning.

"You've created a very cozy atmosphere," I said.

"Do you approve?"

"I'm definitely not complaining."

He then got up and started kissing my neck. Slowly, he started unraveling my veil.

"Is it alright?" he asked timidly.

"Yes," I replied softly.

As he gently took off my scarf, strands of my thick hair cascaded over my robe. He soothingly caressed the dark, curly locks that came down to my lower back. He placed his hands around my waist and started undoing the tie.

"Are you sure this is what you want?" he whispered in my ear.

"I've never wanted anything so badly," I said.

He let the robe fall off my shoulders and he was surprised to see my black, see through, lace teddy. He turned my body towards him.

"You are a goddess. The most beautiful creature I've ever seen," he said as he looked at me with burning desire. We kissed passionately. Then, he started kissing my neck and moved down to my breasts.

"Let's go to my bedroom," he said.

We kept kissing till we stumbled onto the bed. We were both consumed with lust. He smoothly worked his hands up and down my body. I was so turned on and I could feel he was about to burst. He removed my top as he nibbled on my breasts.

"Are you Ok?" he asked.

"I'm in heaven."

He devoured my lips as our bodies became one. It was ecstasy. I had never, ever felt this way. It was truly bliss.

When we were done he asked: "Was it everything you wanted it to be?" as he caressed my hair.

"It was. You made me feel so alive."

"Let's take a warm shower and go to bed. Let me hold you all night."

"I'd like that."

The next morning Brahim surprised me by bringing me breakfast in bed.

"You are too sweet ayunnee," I said.

"For you habeebtee this is not enough," he said.

"You are enough," I said as I insinuated with my kiss that I was ready for another love making session.

That day we stayed in bed all day, we just came out before dusk to keep our promise to the sun. Then, we came back in and just relaxed and listened to Sinatra tapes.

"Brahim, I'd like to ask you something. I don't want you to take it the wrong way. I'll understand if you don't want to talk about it."

"You want to know about Heather?" he said in a nostalgic tone.

"That was her name?"

"Yes. I met her while doing our fellowship. It was love at first sight. I knew she was the love of my life. She was such a giving woman. She always made time for others. She was so compassionate. A brilliant doctor who embodied what the medical field is all about."

"It sounds like she was a marvelous person. What did she look like?"

"She was blonde with blue eyes and a smile that would brighten a room. She made me laugh. Shortly after graduation, we got married. Everything I ever wanted had become a reality. A beautiful wife, my career in medicine, children down the line; I was living the American dream. We were planning a trip to Antarah so she could meet my family. This chalet was going to be my gift to her," he said.

"So, what happened?"

"Three weeks before our trip, she got an emergency call from the hospital. She kissed me goodbye and rushed out. An hour later, they called me to say she never made it to the hospital. She had died instantly in a car accident."

"I'm so sorry, baby," I said, wiping his tears. I was so moved by his story that I couldn't help wiping my own tears. "I had no right to ask you…"

"I wanted to tell you, I just wanted to find the right moment," he said. "I was so devastated by her death. We had so many plans for our life and everything vanished within seconds. I was so haunted by my memories, I just came back home. My family really helped me. I grew closer to God. Allah helped me find my calling in Antarah. So, I went to work at the hospital and you know the rest."

"Ayunnee," I said as I hugged him. "I'm so sorry. I would do anything to take away your pain."

"I never thought I would love again. I thought Heather was the only person who could fill my heart. Then, I met you. You brought hope back into my life; my desire to live. Heather will always be in my heart but now I have you. I love you Fatima, and it hurts to know that I can't have you all to myself. It hurts to know that life is cheating me out of happiness once again."

"You think it's not killing me inside to know that I love you and I can't spend the rest of my life with you. I just want to be with you."

"So, let's run off together. Let's go back to the States," he said.

"What about our commitment to the hospital, the children?"

"What about us?"

"I'm so afraid of Fouad and what he can do to you. I couldn't bear to lose you."

"Let's not rush into anything. Let's give ourselves time to think. Maybe we could work it out somehow," I said. "Let's just enjoy this time as if it were forever. Let's not burden ourselves with what's to come. Please."

"Whatever you say, habeebtee."

"Why don't you come here and show me how much you love me?" I asked.

I felt as if my life had just begun. Every moment with Brahim was a discovery of my feelings. Our nights were filled with passion and desire. He was such a thoughtful lover always putting my needs first. When our bodies came together, we became one, body and soul.

Brahim's tenderness and understanding made me hope that maybe one day we could be free to love each other without hiding from the world.

We had our own ritual when we were together; each day, we watched the Mediterranean sunset. It was as if nature prepared this special spectacle just for us. It was stunning. That sunset was our hope that a tomorrow would come and bring us the life we always dreamed of.

On our fourth night, we made love on the sand under a clear, perfect sky showered with stars. What an amazing experience! Afterwards, we ran naked into the warm ocean water and allowed the gentle motion of the waves to wrap our bodies into a state of ecstasy.

Later that evening, we went inside and talked for hours. Brahim told me about growing up in Antarah: the culture, people, politics and religion. He compared life in the States with life here. It was fascinating to hear him talk and share his points of view.

The good doctor never ceased to amaze me. One afternoon while I showered, I heard the sound of what seemed to be a flute. I thought it was a tape. Instead, he was playing the aspeh, a slim, hollow wooden flute traditional to soft Arabic music.

I decided to surprise him by wearing my belly-dancing outfit. It was a bright purple sequined top with a matching hip belt and a skirt made out of an array of sheer scarves in bright colors. I placed a veil over my hair and secured it with a golden tiara with a purple stone that fell above my nose. I covered my face exposing only my dramatically, made up eyes and sprinkled body glitter on my exposed tanned torso.

When Brahim saw me, he almost dropped the aspeh. Although he had been playing melancholic tunes, he attempted to pick up the beat allowing me to show off my dancing skills. As I uncovered my face and hair, I brushed his face and arms with the veil. It was my first time belly dancing for a man. It felt very exciting as I seduced him while he devoured me with his eyes. Needless to say, it was a passionate night.

Every time we made love, we grew closer. This was a level of intimacy I had never experienced; a closeness that is only reached once in a lifetime with that one special person.

The next morning when I woke up, I realized Brahim wasn't at the chalet. I went for a walk on the beach and let my mind wander. I was totally happy. This was our magical place; a place where we forgot all our troubles and lived for the moment. When I got back, I found a beautifully wrapped box on my bed.

"Brahim!" I shouted.

"Good morning habeebtee," he said as he kissed me. "I see you've found your surprise, open it."

When I opened the box, I saw three, golden bangle bracelets.

"These are gorgeous."

"These will represent our past, our present and our future," he said as he slid them onto my wrist.

"I will never take them off. They will be a part of me just like you will always be a part of me, the most precious part of me. I love you."

"I love you too," he said then kissed me.

It was hard to believe that time had gone by so fast.

"A few more days and we will be leaving …"

"You have another week off, don't you? Come with me to D.C. It will be great. We will stay at my father's house. You will get to see where I grew up. Let me share those memories with you," I said.

"Are you sure you don't want to be alone? Don't you want to visit with friends? Aren't you going to be busy taking care of your father's estate? Won't it be risky?"

"We'll be careful. I just want to be with you. I don't want this feeling to end. Another week together in the States would be amazing."

"I'll go with you."

I wrapped myself around him and kissed him.

"Thank you, sweetie," I said.

For the next few days we wondered if our trip to D.C. would bring us closer to the truth about Fouad. We hoped my father had left some clues or concrete information that would uncover the secrets behind my marriage.

Our last Mediterranean sunset was memorable in many ways. The area had been isolated the entire week. On this particular evening, we heard someone shouting for help. I immediately covered my face. Brahim and I rushed to see what was wrong.

"My son… He's in the water. He can't swim; I can't swim," he said in despair.

Brahim rushed into the water and brought the child's lifeless body to shore.

"Is he dead?" the man said crying.

"He's a doctor," I said. "He will do whatever it takes to save him."

Brahim started aggressively performing C.P.R. It was déjà vu. I remembered how he tried to save my father's life unsuccessfully. I prayed this time would have a different outcome. Suddenly, water came out of the child's mouth. He was alive. I ran to the chalet to get his medical bag. Brahim checked his vital signs and everything seemed to be fine.

"You scared your father to death," the man told his son as he hugged him then turned to Brahim. "Thank you for saving my son's life, doctor."

"Ibrahim Al-Kateb," he said extending his hand.

"Ramsey Janoudi at your service," the man said shaking Brahim's hand.

Unexpectedly, a strong breeze blew my scarf exposing my face. The man looked at me as if he recognized me.

"How are you feeling?" Brahim asked the child.

"O.K., I guess," the boy said.

"What's your name?" Brahim asked.

"Bilal," he replied

"Bilal, you gave your father a big scare. You have to be very careful. The currents are strong this time of the year. You shouldn't stray from your father if neither one of you can swim well."

"I'm really sorry, Baba. Thanks for saving my life, Dr. Ibrahim," the boy said.

"If your wife or you ever need anything, you can find me at the eastern border checkpoint office. Just ask for Lieutenant Janoudi," the man said.

At that moment, I excused myself and returned to the chalet. Brahim followed shortly after.

"I think that man recognized me. I don't know him but I sensed he knew who I was," I said nervously.

"Fatima, relax. Even if he does know you, I think he feels indebted to us. I don't think he would say anything unless he was one hundred percent certain. Just let it go. I don't want you worrying about this."

"Just hold me tight."

chapter 19

A Trip To D.C.

We left the chalet before dawn and headed to our next adventure: Washington D.C. We decided not to sit side by side on the plane. It was best to keep our distance. Before arriving to D.C., we had arranged to take separate cabs and meet at my house. That way no one could make any connection between us. It was a long, lonely trip but we knew it would pay off with another five days of loving each other without constantly looking over our shoulders.

The house looked just like it had on the day I left. Everything was in its place. As per my request, the refrigerator had been fully stocked and the pool was pristine. It felt great being back home. When Brahim arrived, I showed him around. He was very impressed with what he saw.

"And this is my room…" I said.

"Nice," he replied.

"Nothing has changed except for the fact that this is the first time a man, other than my father, has been in my room."

"Well, let's make this first time unforgettable," he said as he started to undress me.

"I missed you so much," I said. "That plane ride seemed to drag on for forever."

"I couldn't wait to hold you again."

It felt odd making love in my old bedroom; the same bedroom where I had envisioned my future life with the man of my dreams. Brahim was the realization of those dreams. Now, we were both here sharing an incredible moment.

After our blissful encounter, we showered together and went downstairs in our robes. I proceeded to disrobe his chest area and rub his shoulders with oil.

"So, how does it feel being back in the States?" I asked.

"I haven't given it much thought. Being with you is all I care about no matter where we are. This back rub is just what the doctor ordered."

"The doctor's order is my command. You know, there is something I already miss from back home…our Mediterranean sunsets," I said.

"Me too," he said as he grabbed my body, sat me on his lap and kissed my lips. "Our sunsets will always be waiting for us, though. We'll return to the chalet soon enough."

That evening we ordered Chinese food and watched television. We fell asleep on the sofa in each other's arms, exhausted after a grueling day of travel.

The next morning I woke him up with a kiss.

"Good morning, sleepy head."

"Good morning, habeebtee."

"I have to meet with my father's attorney this morning, but after that the day is ours. Ayunnee, what are your plans?

"Oh, just watch some television, catch up on my soaps..." he said laughing.

"Be ready by noon and we'll take in the sights."

"I'll be ready."

"Please don't open the door for anyone. I told the attorney not to have the realtor show the house this week. So, no one should be coming around. Sorry, I have to rush. I love you," I said kissing him good- bye.

"I love you too, baby. Have a good day," he replied.

As I drove to see the lawyer, I just wished Baba and Mama were alive to see how happy I was. In a way, it was comforting to know that my father had met Brahim, if only that one night. I could tell by my father's body language that he liked him, even though their encounter was brief.

I anticipated the meeting at the law office not to be long. I knew we would be discussing the will. My father had the D.C. home, a car, and a life insurance policy. I had always thought of my father as a lavish spender. Hence, I expected to use some of the money from the insurance policy to pay whatever debts he had incurred. His legacy to me was our home; the place where we made our memories, where I grew up, where I spent the last moments with my mother. Nothing else mattered. Although I had always lived a comfortable life, money wasn't a priority. I would give up all my wealth just to spend my life with Brahim; if it were only that easy.

"Did my father leave a letter addressed to me?" I asked impatiently.

"No," the attorney responded. "All I have is his last will and testament, which he updated right before going to visit you. I remember he was very anxious to see you."

"No keys to a safe...?"

"I'm afraid not. Only the papers in front of me."

"Let's get down to business then."

As he started reading, all the special moments with my father flashed before my eyes. I tried to be strong, but I couldn't avoid wiping the tears that rolled down my cheeks until something the attorney said made me pause.

"… and my villa in Tuscany, Italy, the money in my three international bank accounts, totaling over 20 million dollars, and all money from a list of overseas investments…" the attorney read.

"Stop," I said baffled. "Is this a joke?"

"No, Ms. Aziz. Your father was a very wealthy man."

"An ambassador's salary could not provide all this, especially the way he used to throw away his money."

"I don't know what to tell you, but your father had always invested his money to guarantee you and your mother's well being. After your mother's passing, he made sure that you would become a very wealthy woman. He also stipulated the sum of one million dollars over a period of 5 years for Ms. Jamila Musa, whom he loved like a daughter."

"Did my father ever discuss my husband Fouad with you? Did Fouad know what he could expect to gain?"

"The subject of your husband never came up."

"I just don't understand how my father accumulated such a fortune and how I was kept in the dark until now."

"You are a fortunate woman," the attorney said.

"If only wealth could buy happiness…"

I left with more questions than answers. I had always seen my father as a diplomat, not a businessman. I couldn't grasp the idea that he had earned this fortune. I had many doubts regarding how he made his money. I wondered if Fouad knew about his wealth. Furthermore, did Fouad know the secrets behind it? What was the connection, if any?

When I got back to the house, I ran into Brahim's arms.

"What's wrong?" he asked.

"Everything," I said.

"What happened at the lawyer's?"

"I found out that I'm very well off, and my gut tells me that the money wasn't all hard earned cash."

"I don't know what to say. You know God has a plan for all of us. Just think about the great things you can do to help others.

This can be a true blessing."

"Or a curse…I'm sorry, you're right. I'm just so confused. I have doubts about how my father came into his fortune. I even have the crazy idea that Fouad has known about this all along."

"That he married you for your money?"

"Wouldn't be the first man to do so."

"Isn't he well off? I'm sure he is in a position to become a very wealthy man."

"You don't know Fouad. For someone like him, there is never enough money. I could be his added insurance policy."

"Did the attorney bring Fouad up in conversation?"

"I brought him up. The attorney said my father never discussed him. The only other person who was brought up was Jamila. She has been like a sister to me."

"Maybe Fouad is unaware of your father's business affairs."

"Let's get out of here. I need some fresh air. I don't want to think anymore."

We took my father's car and a camera. I wanted to document our trip. I put all my troubles aside for that afternoon. I let my hair down, literally, and decided not to wear my scarf while we were on vacation. Brahim didn't mind me showing off my hair. He felt it was a personal decision and left it up to me. I just wanted to feel free in every way like the good old days: the days when it would never have crossed my mind that my father could be involved in criminal activities.

We drove for a while then went to the Washington Monument and both the Lincoln and Vietnam Memorials. We also rode the carousel at the National Mall. During the next few days, we went to the White House, the U.S. Capitol, the Jefferson Memorial, the National Gallery of Art and the Kennedy Center. I had visited all of these places with my father as a child and, now as an adult, I was reliving my memories with Brahim. Our days were filled with activities. I wanted Brahim to enjoy himself and get to know me more by sharing a piece of my history with him. I also wanted to escape all my negative thoughts; my fears of discovering that my father wasn't who I thought he was.

One afternoon, I packed a picnic basket and we went to the Great Falls of the Potomac; it was a spectacular sight. After lunch, we rented a couple of bicycles and hit the trails along the river. We were having a lovely time getting to know each other day by day. Every once in a while, we would stop someone and ask them to take our picture.

"Are you enjoying yourself so far?" I asked.

"You're a great tour guide. D.C. is a great place. There are so many things to do. I truly wish we could stay longer," he said.

"I know. First, the chalet and now D.C. We've had some amazing moments in such a short time."

"This is a taste of what our life could be like if we take a chance."

"We have to keep looking for anything that could help set me free. No one wants this more than I do."

"I love you Fatme, and I can't bear to let you go."

"I'm not going anywhere. I will always be by your side."

We kissed like it was the first time. We kissed for so long that we lost track of time. We kissed with the intensity of two lovers that fear that if they stop, they will wake up and realize it was all a dream.

Every night, we would turn the house upside down, room by room, hoping to find answers. The closest we got was finding one of my father's planners with some ripped out pages that might have uncovered the information we desperately wanted to find. We were very frustrated but didn't give up hope.

On our last evening in town, I made reservations at The Prime Rib. It was a restaurant where my parents used to go on their special dates. They shared this romantic spot with me when I was in my teens. Today, I wanted to share it with Brahim.

When we got home late afternoon, Brahim surprised me with a gift. When I opened the exquisitely wrapped box, I found a pale pink gown.

"I've never seen you in light colors. I thought pink would set off your olive skin and dark eyes, making you glow." When he saw my expression, he paused. "Did I say something wrong?" he said, wiping my tears.

"This was the color of my sweet sixteen dress. It was a magical evening. All these memories of my father just came rushing through my head when I saw the dress. It is truly beautiful. You're so thoughtful. Thank you," I said giving him a tight hug.

"When did you have the time…?"

"A man has to have some secrets."

"I'll leave you to your secrets while I get ready."

When I saw him again, he was wearing a black pin-striped suit with a French blue shirt and a silk tie with pale pink stripes. My gown fit like a glove. We looked fabulous.

Before we left the house, I set the camera on a tripod and finished the film. On our way to dinner, I dropped it at a one-hour photo place to guarantee the pictures would be ready in the morning.

When we walked into the restaurant, Oscar, the maître d', greeted us. He had worked there for over twenty years. He immediately recognized me and offered his condolences. Oscar had always been very fond of my father and was extremely discrete.

It was crazy being in public like this, on a date, taking the chance of running into someone we knew. But we were thousands of miles away from Antarah, and just wanted to be a normal couple.

Everything looked the same. The dramatic leopard-spotted carpet, the massive flower arrangements, the black and gold accents, and my parent's usual table in a very secluded corner. It all brought back so many memories. The pianist sitting at the baby grand and the bass player were enjoying themselves creating the right mood for lovers like the good old times.

"How do you like the place?" I asked.

"It's as you described. I can see why your parents came here on special occasions. Love is in the air. And, in case I forgot to tell you, you look radiant tonight," he said.

"You've only told me like a million times, but I love hearing it. Thank you, ayunnee."

The waiter brought us the menu and some mineral water. Oscar had already warned him not to bother with the wine list because we didn't drink.

We began with oysters and worked our way through a four-course meal. At one point during dinner, Brahim approached the musicians. Minutes later they were delighting us with some Sinatra classics. "Fly me to the Moon" played in the background while we sensually fed each other. Between bites, I would remove one of my shoes and stroke him between the legs until he got aroused It was a very stimulating game, anticipating what would happen later that night.

"I hope you're ready for tonight, you know what they say about oysters," he said as he excused himself to use the restroom.

"I'm sure it's all true," I said as he walked away.

Seconds later a voice called out my name.

"Fatima?"

I turned my head.

"Rauf, what are you doing here?" I asked in disbelief.

"I could ask you the same thing," Rauf said.

"I'm in D.C. taking care of my father's estate," I told him.

"My father wanted me to check on the embassy, to make sure the transition for the new ambassador was going smoothly. How long are you staying?"

At this point, I prayed that Brahim would catch on to what was happening. I saw him starting to approach the table.

"I'm leaving tomorrow morning," I said.

When I looked up, I realized Brahim was gone.

"I was hoping we could spend some time together," Rauf said.

"You know that wouldn't be appropriate."

"We're friends aren't we?"

"Technically, I'm your best friend's wife. I don't think he would approve of us socializing without him present."

"Where's your dinner date?" Rauf asked when he noticed a second placing.

"She left," I quickly replied.

"You are all dressed up for a she?"

"Fouad is certainly not here and I'm sure you're not implying I'm here with a man," I said, acting a bit upset.

"I'm sorry if I offended you," Rauf said apologetic. "May I join you?"

"I'm actually getting ready to leave. My plane takes off early in the morning."

"Indulge me."

As he got closer to me, I smelled liquor on his breath.

"How about a cup of coffee, Rauf?" I asked.

"Waiter, a cup of coffee for the lady and a scotch on the rocks for me," Rauf said. "So, what are you doing for the rest of the evening?" he asked, holding my hand.

"Packing," I said in a sharp tone, removing his hand from mine.

"You know, Fouad would be very upset if he knew you were out in public without your scarf."

"I would appreciate it if you didn't mention it."

"You are even more beautiful than I imagined. How did Fouad get so damn lucky?" he asked, as he sipped his drink.

"Rauf, you're drunk. Why don't I call you a cab?"

Seconds later, a young woman approached the table.

"Rauf, I've been looking all over for you," she said.

"Missy, this is my best friend's wife, Fatima," he said.

"Nice meeting you," the woman said.

"Likewise. I have to go. Please, make sure he doesn't drive. I think he's had a little too much to drink. Bye Rauf, Missy."

"Fatima, your secret is safe with me," Rauf said.

As I walked off, I wondered if Rauf was referring only to the scarf or if he had seen Brahim. I was very troubled by his remark. The maître d' informed me that my companion had paid the bill and left. I took a taxi home. When I arrived, Brahim was outside.

"I'm so sorry for what happened," I said.

"Was that Rauf?" he asked.

"Yes, he's in D.C. on official business," I said as I opened the door.

"Does his official business include making a pass at you?" he asked sarcastically.

"Rauf is a big flirt. Besides, he was drunk. Are you jealous?"

"What if I am?"

"Rauf is a self proclaimed playboy. He might have a little crush on me because I'm forbidden fruit, but he knows his boundaries. Nothing to worry about, my heart belongs only to you. You're so sexy when you're jealous."

He pulled me tight against his body.

"You like to play games, don't you?" he asked as he teased me with kisses.

"I like you to be protective of me. By the way, weren't you telling me something about oysters earlier?"

"I'm glad you brought it up," he said leading my hand below his belt. "Do you like this?" he said as he kissed my neck and started to unzip my dress.

"My, my, I thought what they said about oysters was just wishful thinking. I guess I was wrong," I said as I undid his tie and unbuttoned his shirt.

I don't know if it was the oysters or the incident with Rauf but something made me more desirable that evening. Brahim was on fire; we made love all night long. He made sure to let me know that I was only his.

When morning came, I went to pick up the photographs. As I looked at them, I smiled. The lens had captured every delicious moment we were together. Suddenly, I was sad because I knew that we were going back to living a lie and I didn't know how much longer Brahim could really cope with this farce. Now, everything seemed ideal because

Fouad was out of the picture. But when Fouad came back, I knew Brahim would not stand the thought of another man touching me. I couldn't stand the idea of being touched by another man.

Brahim loved the pictures. We both kept one to remember our amazing time together. The rest were stored in a hidden safe that only my father and I knew about. It was even risky carrying that one photograph but we needed to have something to hold on to.

We slept for most of the trip back to Antarah. We were exhausted from such an intense week and such passionate nights. The long journey also provided too much time to think about my father and the obscene amount of cash he had left behind. My mind concocted all the worst case scenarios. I felt betrayed by his past life and guilty for jumping to conclusions.

When we finally arrived, we went our separate ways. That night,

I slept with our picture under my pillow. I just wanted to feel close to him.

chapter 20

Business As Usual

The next time I saw him was the following day at work. Dalal was with me.

"Good morning, doctor," I said.

"Welcome back," Dalal said.

"I understand you were on vacation. Did you have a good time?" I asked him hoping Dalal would not make any connection considering we were out at the same time.

"It was very relaxing. How's the baby?" he asked turning to Dalal.

"Big and beautiful, thanks for asking. You look rested," Dalal said.

"So, are you ready to get back to work on our project?" I asked.

"Most definitely," he answered.

"I'll pass by your office later," I said as he walked away.

"So, tell me about your trip," Dalal said.

"It was nice being back in D.C. I was saddened by the memories, but at the same time I remembered many wonderful times we spent at the house. I did a little sightseeing, laid by the pool. Just took it easy."

"Did you miss Dr. Ibrahim?" she asked.

"I thought about him a few times, but I was busy taking care of things, and there is no point in fantasizing about something that's never going to happen."

"I guess at this point you are better off steering clear of trouble," Dalal said.

"Yes, I have my hands full as it is."

Little did she know I was already way over my head in a relationship with the doctor. I decided I wouldn't share all the things that happened to me with any of my friends, especially Dalal or Jamila. The less they knew, the better off they would be. I didn't want them to become accomplices to my sins if Fouad ever found out.

"Have you heard from Fouad?" Dalal asked.

"No," I said indifferently.

"Dalal, I need to take these papers to Dr. Ibrahim. Can we talk later?"

"Sure."

I couldn't stand a minute longer without feeling Brahim's touch. I rushed to his office right before he was heading to surgery.

"Hi," I said, locking the door behind me.

"Come here, habeebtee," he said.

"I couldn't sleep all night, thinking about you."

We kissed passionately.

"I couldn't sleep, either. I need to be with you," he said.

"They're waiting for you in surgery. Go. Find me when you are finished. I'll be thinking about you."

"Me too," he said kissing my forehead.

Every hour that passed seemed like forever. I was having a hard time concentrating. All I could think about was our next time at the chalet.

Three hours later, we were back in my office.

"We have to stop meeting this way," he said kissing the back of my neck.

"I know," I said as I turned to face him. "I missed you all day."

"Where can we meet to be alone?"

"I don't know. We might have to wait till the end of the week, when we go back to the chalet."

"I don't think I can wait that long."

"Meet me back here this evening," I said. "I'll work late, and when everyone leaves, you can drop by."

It was a little past seven. Everyone from the day shift was gone, and I was impatiently waiting for Brahim. I heard a soft knock on the door.

"Come in," I said. "I've been waiting."

He locked the door and walked up to me. He pinned me against the wall with one hand and started kissing my face, neck and breasts while rubbing my body with his other hand. Then, he slid his hand under my skirt and proceeded to take off my panties and give me pleasure. As I moaned in ecstasy, he pulled me up and placed me on the cold, steel desk. I carefully unzipped his pants, pulled down his underwear and squeezed his naked buttocks, as he penetrated me. It was simultaneous gratification.

Maybe it was the excitement generated by the idea that someone could walk in on us, but our lovemaking was out of this world and was only getting better.

"Wow, how do you manage to make me feel this way?" he asked.

"I could ask you the same thing," I said.

"When we make love, it's magical. I can't get enough of you."

"I feel the same way."

We held each other for a few minutes and got dressed. I opened the door slowly to make sure that the area was clear for him to leave. Afterwards, I went home and daydreamed about our lovemaking.

We promised there would be no more physical encounters until that weekend at the chalet. It was a rough week, but each day we learned to restrain our feelings and be thankful that we had a place to be together again.

That same week, I received a letter from Fouad, the first one in two months. He wrote everything a woman separated from her husband for months would want to hear; how he missed me, couldn't wait to see me and hold me in his arms, and how much he needed and wanted me. It made me sick to my stomach. The only reason I read it was to make sure Rauf had kept his promise of not mentioning our D.C. encounter.

He was probably so embarrassed over his drunken behavior that he decided to forget that evening ever happened.

I finally went to visit Jamila. I had neglected our friendship since my involvement with the hospital and Brahim. It was just so difficult being around her and not being able to open up about everything like we used to. I also missed little Ramee. He had grown so much.

"Hello, stranger," Jamila said as she gave me a big hug. "I've missed you."

"I'm sorry. I know I've been a rotten friend but I've been so caught up in work, then the trip to Washington…" I said.

"Apology accepted. How was it, going back to D.C?" Jamila asked.

"Strange and wonderful at the same time. I was sad but all my memories filled me with joy. The best part was learning about the surprise my father left for you."

"For me?"

"You know he loved you like a daughter. Here, this is the first of five yearly installments," I said handing her a check.

"There has to be a mistake. This is a lot of money."

"And it's all yours. Enjoy."

"This can't be. Oh my God!" she started crying. "This is a miracle."

"I'm so happy my father shared some of his wealth with you. I have also established a trust fund for Ramee and all the other babies that will follow. You have no need to worry about their future. It's all taken care of. Use this money for you and Nabil. Go on a trip, buy another home… Remember there is another check like this one coming every year for the next four years."

"This is enough for all of us."

"Just allow me to do this for Ramee and his siblings. I love you and I'm in a position to do this. Don't fight me. Just know that you will have no more financial worries."

Jamila hugged me tight and told me she was already expecting her second child. This was wonderful news. She told me that her relationship with Nabil was everything she had ever dreamed it would be. I was so happy for them. For the first time, I could relate to this feeling of total fulfillment.

"I have to ask, how are things between you and Fouad?"

"Great, now that he is out of town."

"Seriously."

"I am serious. My relationship with Fouad is a dead end. I can't accept his infidelities and he's not willing to change."

"Yet, you seem so happy. Is anything going on that I should know about? Have you done something crazy?"

"Of course not. How could I? Even if I wanted, it would be too dangerous. I've just made peace with my situation."

"You had me worried for a second."

This was another reason why my discretion was crucial. I couldn't have her worrying about me, and I couldn't take the chance that she would discuss my situation with her husband. My behavior might jeopardize our friendship and even endanger their lives. That was too big of a risk. After several hours of talking with Jamila and playing with Ramee, I went home.

The visit had been a much needed distraction. The rest of the evening I thought about Brahim and gazed at our picture in anticipation of our next encounter. I fell asleep and couldn't help waking up the next day with a smile on my face.

chapter 21

A Family Affair

The weekend was finally here and I was on my way to meet Brahim at our love nest. We arrived separately. Brahim arrived at the chalet before me. Trails of rose petals led me to the bedroom, where an exquisite piece of lingerie was laid over the bed with a note that read, "This will be an unforgettable day." In the bathroom, a warm bubble bath surrounded by candles awaited me. I undressed and soaked as I heard his steps. With his hair slicked back, his body concealed in a robe, the fresh, clean smell of aftershave surrounding him, he kneeled down and started kissing my neck as he scrubbed my back.

"I missed you so much," he whispered in my ear.

"I missed you more, my love," I replied.

As the water drained, I stood up and he gently dried every inch of my body. I excused myself to slip into a soft, silky nightgown that made me feel like royalty for the few seconds it was on my body.

This prelude to the inevitable had just made our desires uncontrollable. Yet, we showed restraint and played out the fantasy as Brahim kissed my body from my little toe to the tip of my forehead. I eventually lost control, flipped him over and started making love to him until we both climaxed.

"You were incredible," he said as I put my head over his chest while I listened to his heartbeat.

"Well, you did say this was going to be an unforgettable day."

"That was an understatement. You were on fire, and I just love to feel that uninhibited passion."

"You are the only one who can unleash these feelings that I never knew I had," I said kissing his chest.

"Those feelings are love. When we come together, we become one. You complete me in every way. I love you, Fatme," he said as he lifted my head and brought our lips together in a kiss. "Tonight, I want you to look radiant. I have a surprise for you."

"Give me a clue."

"Be patient."

That afternoon, Brahim told me we would be going out. After our Mediterranean sunset ritual, we went back to the house where he surprised me with a beautiful outfit. I got dressed and concealed my

identity before stepping out. Twenty minutes later, we arrived to a house.

"Where are we?" I asked.

"You are safe here," he said.

An older lady opened the door.

"Habeebee Brahim," she said kissing him.

"Mama, this is Fatima," he said.

"Ajala usajala, welcome."

She greeted me with kisses and walked me into a house full of family.

"She is even more beautiful than you described."

"Fatima, this is my family," he said.

I was truly overwhelmed. There were at least 20 people, all strangers to me but I felt at home. They were all so attentive, so nice. The women immediately pulled me to the side to sing Brahim's praises. Minutes later, his mother took me by the hand and into the kitchen where we sat down.

"Fatme, thanks for making my son's eyes sparkle again and for putting a smile back on his face. You have given him a reason for living," she said with tears in her eyes.

"No tears, Mama," Brahim said as he walked in and wiped her face. "Today is a happy day," he said, kissing her forehead.

"My wonderful son, thank you for sharing this sweet girl with us," she said looking at me.

While his mother put the final touches to a home cooked feast, I spoke to Brahim.

"What have you told them?" I asked.

"Only what they need to know," he replied. "That I'm in love, that you are the love of my life..."

"How about the part about me being married?" I asked whispering as we moved outside.

"I didn't want to burden them with the unpleasant details but I think my parents suspect."

"What makes you think that?"

"They haven't asked many questions."

"I really don't know what to say. I'm thrilled and honored to be with your family, but I don't know if I could stand their rejection when they find out the truth. I don't want to be judged, but I would understand if they did. You deserve so much better. I have so much baggage..." I said as he softly kissed my lips.

"I brought you here because I love you. I'm proud of you and I want to share you with the ones closest to me. I know they will accept you with open arms. Let all your insecurities go and live for the moment. They already love you," he said holding my hand and leading me into the dining room with a table full of Arabic delights.

"Masha Allah," I said.

His mother grabbed me by the arm and handed me a plate so I could serve myself.

"Don't be shy. Eat as much as you want. This is your home," his mom insisted.

Brahim then followed and the rest of the family joined in on the banquet.

"It is delicious. You are an excellent cook," I said.

"I can't take all of the credit. Abu Jamal, Brahim's father, also helped," his mom said.

"Like father like son," I replied. "Brahim gets his love for cooking from both sides of the family."

"As a child, Abu Hasan always came to help us in the kitchen. He would gather all the ingredients and help me assemble the dishes," his father added.

"Abu Hasan," I thought to myself.

Abu Hasan, father of Hasan, which meant Brahim's father's name was Hasan. Traditionally his sons would call their first-born son Hasan. Hence, Brahim and his male brothers are nicknamed Abu Hasan in anticipation of that son.

It was only logical to drift off and imagine that I would bear Brahim's first-born son, Hasan, which means handsome, beautiful. My ideal future flashed before my eyes: the birth of Hasan, the happiness of our family, watching our son and our love grow...

"Where were you just now?" Brahim asked as he snapped me out of it.

"I was envisioning our future," I replied.

"How was it?" he asked.

"Full of joy, hope and more love than I ever imagined possible," I said.

After dinner, Brahim's mom brought out his first aspeh and insisted that he play. Everyone sat outside in the courtyard to listen to the melancholic sound of this native instrument. It was as if the sad melody narrated the story of our forbidden love; a love eager to grow yet destined to wither.

Tears rolled down his mother's eyes as she proudly listened to her son display one of his many talents. I remembered my mother and the way she looked at me. I couldn't help being deeply touched by the moment.

After a few songs, Brahim's father put an end to the gloomy mood and broke out a more cheerful instrument to play dancing music. The party really livened up. Brahim's brothers and sisters jumped out of their seats and started dancing while the others clapped. Brahim insisted I get up and join in the dancing. We had many laughs. The evening was a total success. I seemed to fit right in. I felt very comfortable with all of them.

When we said our goodbyes, Brahim's mom insisted that I come back soon, with or without her son, adding that I was always welcome at their home. I sensed Brahim was very pleased with the way his family embraced me.

"That wasn't so bad was it?" he asked.

"I really had a great time, thank you," I said. "I haven't felt that family closeness since my D.C. days."

When we got back to the chalet, we changed into something comfy and walked on the beach. We exchanged family stories; we spoke about our parents and everything they had done and sacrificed for us. We pondered about our lives and where we were headed. I even shared my dreams about baby Hasan. This really warmed Brahim's heart.

"If it's a girl we will call her Iman, in memory of your mother," he said.

"That's so sweet, I'd like that very much," I said.

We sat on the damp sand for countless hours, talking and holding each other until the sun rose. It was a glorious beginning to a new day. The only dark cloud in the horizon was Fouad's existence; an inevitable reality that would put a damper on our ability to live out our dreams.

That afternoon, I told Brahim that I wanted to go back to his parents' house. I felt he had been neglecting his family ever since we started seeing each other, and it was important for both of us to spend time with them. Brahim was delighted that I wanted to share our special time with his family.

"Tell your mom just for a cup of tea; nothing fancy. They did enough yesterday," I shouted as he walked toward the phone.

When we arrived to his parents' house, they had a table full of fruit, salad, and trays of Arabic pastries. The simple set up was a meal in itself. From the moment we got there till the moment we left, his parents and siblings kept trying to feed us and we loved every bite.

"We were so happy when Brahim called saying you were on your way," his mom said.

"I'm touched by your hospitality," I said.

"Brahim has told us about all the wonderful projects you have developed as a team," his father added.

"We've been very fortunate to obtain the funding for the clinics," I replied.

"You are doing such great work especially for the children. God will bless you for this labor of love," his mom said.

"I couldn't have done it without Brahim's support. He involved all his colleagues in the project and that was an integral part of its success."

"We are proud of both of you," his father said.

At the end of the evening, I insisted on helping with the dishes.

"I feel so at home with your family," I told his mom.

"We feel like you are part of our family," she said.

"After my father died, I thought I would never feel this sense of belonging, but you've changed all that. Thank you," I said as tears rolled down my face.

"Don't cry Fatme, you are like a daughter to me," she said.

"And you are like a mother to me," I said as we hugged.

The kitchen door swung open. "Am I interrupting?" Brahim asked.

"Just girl talk," I said.

I was glad Brahim's mom and I had that time to bond. I felt so comfortable around his family. I now had two reasons to anxiously await my days off: being with Brahim and spending time with his family.

The following weeks were very special. Once a week, Brahim and I got to volunteer at some of the clinics we had helped establish. It was wonderful seeing how our project had taken a life of its own. It was rewarding to see how the neighborhoods embraced our work and how the people seemed more aware of their health. Parents were bringing their children for their scheduled shots and taking preventive measures for their well being. On a personal level, it was also rewarding; this day gave us an excuse to spend an extra night away from home and together.

"Fouad's absence is becoming. You look amazing," Dalal said.

"A stress free life is rejuvenating," I said.

"By the way, how are you managing working so closely with Dr. Ibrahim once a week?" Dalal asked.

"Just fine. We are so proud of the work that is being done at the clinics."

"How about your unresolved feelings?"

"That's a thing of the past."

"How about his feelings? I see how he looks at you."

"He's just a flirt. Everything is under control. We are just colleagues nothing more."

"Good for you. I would hate to see you get hurt."

I hated lying to her. I was often tempted to tell her how much we loved each other, but I couldn't do it. I missed having a girlfriend to chat with, but Dalal and Jamila could not be involved.

The next couple of months were so rewarding. I had grown close to Brahim's family and missed them almost as much as I missed him. They had become my surrogate family, and I really felt like a part of their clan. I was especially close to his mother. I was ashamed that our situation wasn't what a mother would want for her son, but she never rejected or judged me. She loved me unconditionally.

One particular afternoon, I told Brahim to drop me off at his mom's while he ran some errands. When I saw her, I gave her a big hug and kissed her on each cheek.

"I feel so at peace in this house. You have given me so much love and warmth," I said.

"Fatme, we love you like our own," she said.

"I care for your son so much. He has taught me the meaning of love and I have you to thank for that; for giving life to the most wonderful human being I've ever known," I said with tears in my eyes.

Minutes later, I took off my mother's bracelet with the locket. I had put a picture of Brahim's face over the one of my father and me.

"I want you to have this. My mother gave it to me before she died. Now, it is yours because you are the closest I have to a mother. Brahim has told me of all the sacrifices you have made for your children and all the love you've always had for everyone. I would be honored if you accept my gift. This heart has witnessed true love and you are a giver of pure love."

"Habeebtee," she said as tears came out. "You don't have to give me anything. Knowing Brahim is happy, is enough."

She opened the locket and saw the picture. She then kissed it and kissed me.

"This is the loveliest gift anyone has ever given me. You are truly a gem."

I hugged her tight. Our bond was stronger than ever. It was probably a mistake to build this perfect world around me that was never going to last. I needed so much to belong and feel loved that I was falling in my own trap.

Things between Brahim and I were so good. I had almost forgotten I was married to Fouad and that he would be coming home soon. Sometimes, I worried we were getting too comfortable with each other and taking unnecessary risks.

One afternoon, we left together from the hospital and had lunch at an outdoor cafe. We weren't being affectionate in public but our body language spoke for itself. I had the uneasy feeling that someone was watching us.

"Just relax and enjoy the food," Brahim said. "To any observer, we are just two people having lunch."

Still, I knew that despite the distance, Fouad could not be trusted. I hadn't heard from him in a while which made me even more suspicious. I never attempted to contact him or send him any messages with Rauf, which was probably a mistake. Fouad thrived on the idea of controlling me and my lack of communication could only mean that I was enjoying my independence; we were growing apart.

Miles away at a remote military operations facility...

"Esmaa, how are things going?" Fouad said.

"Hello, love! It feels great to be home. Guess who I saw?" Esmaa asked.

"Fatima? Please, tell me she didn't see you."

"Relax, she didn't. I guess while the cat's away…"

"What are you trying to say? Was she with someone?"

"Don't get agitated, we don't want your blood pressure going up."

"Don't play games Esmaa, I know you."

"Don't tell me you are jealous, my dear Fouad? Well, maybe you should be. She was having lunch with a very handsome man. They looked pretty cozy."

"Maybe it was a business lunch."

"I don't think so."

"Were they touching, kissing? Sharmuta, whore!" Fouad shouted in anger.

"If I didn't know you any better I would think you are jealous."

"I'm not going to have her ruining my reputation and playing me for a fool in public."

"I guess your perfect princess isn't that perfect after all. I know your pride is hurt darling but get over it. Don't forget that we have an arrangement. No one, not even your precious Fatima, is going to come between us. But, for your own peace of mind, I'll do some more meddling."

"It is imperative for Fatima not to suspect she is being followed especially by you. Don't let anyone know you are back. I need you to break in the house, when she is not around, and find any documents pertaining to her father's will. Call me as soon as you find something out and Esmaa, I already miss you."

"I'll make my absence worth your while," Esmaa said before hanging up the phone.

After my lunch with Brahim, I headed to the office to wrap up some unfinished business. When I got home, I ate a light dinner and got ready for bed. That evening, as I was lying in bed thinking about my love, the phone rang.

"Hello," I said.

"Good evening, dear," he said.

"Fouad."

"Surprised to hear from me?"

"A little, I guess."

"Have you missed me as much as I've missed you?"

"Probably more," I said as I rolled my eyes.

"Are you in bed?" he asked. "What are you wearing? Do you remember when we made love in my study?"

He kept going on with all these explicit details of one of our sexual encounters.

"Are you getting aroused?" he asked.

"How can I not?" I had to play along.

I could hear his heavy breathing and in return, I pretended the whole thing was turning me on. In reality, I just wanted to hang up and dream about Brahim. When he finally climaxed, I faked a few moans and assured him I couldn't wait for us to be together again. Although nothing had happened between us physically, I felt dirty.

"It's been too long, baby. When are you coming home?" I asked.

"Sooner than you think."

Distance Between Lovers

My days of bliss were coming to an end. I wasn't prepared to have Fouad in my bed. The thought of it disgusted me. How was I going to avoid my husband's advances? How was I going to make time for Brahim? I wasn't able to sleep at night, thinking about what I had gotten myself into. The next morning, I went to Brahim's office.

"We have to talk," I said.

"What's wrong?" he asked.

"Fouad, that's what's wrong. He called last night and implied that he was coming home sooner than expected. What's going to happen to us?" I asked as I walked into his arms and held him tight.

"Habeebtee, let's just leave Antarah right now."

"He will find us. Fouad has too many resources. When he finds us, he'll kill us. I won't jeopardize your life, and I will not live in fear for the rest of my life."

"So, what are you saying? You want to end this?"

"I'm terrified. Maybe we didn't think this through. Maybe we should end this. I don't know how much longer I can live this lie. We can never be together, and I should have known that this was a mistake before dragging you into this mess."

"I knew what I was doing. I knew there would be consequences. I'm not willing to give up on our love, and I never thought that you would. I understand your fears, but I've told you that you're not alone. I'm here to protect you."

"Who's going to protect you? And, how can you protect me when Fouad gets back? What if I never see you again? I need to think. I need some…"

"Space? I'm not going anywhere. I know you're afraid. I hear what you're saying and I'm willing to risk it all for our future, but I can't do it alone. You have to take a stance and not look back. When you're ready, I'll be here."

That afternoon, without Brahim knowing, I requested a week off to visit the clinics and make sure everything was running smoothly. I needed some distance between Brahim and myself. I missed him so much it hurt, but I didn't know what else to do. I met with the community and made sure that they were bringing their children to get immunized and handed out leaflets explaining the importance of preventing illnesses. I felt useful. The people would invite me for coffee or tea at their homes, and I would keep emphasizing the importance of preventive medicine and good eating habits. I spent many hours teaching children how to brush their teeth, how to clean their ears, and how to stay healthy. I kept myself busy trying to forget my pain.

After my last clinic visit, I said my goodbyes and was ready to head home when Brahim pulled up.

"Get in the car," Brahim said.

"What are you doing here?" I asked.

"I came to pick you up to go to the chalet."

"Why are you doing this?"

"Give me one more sunset. If after our night together you want to call it quits, I'll respect your decision."

On our way to the chalet, I was very quiet. I knew this was a mistake. I needed to be strong, but I couldn't. I loved him too much.

It was early afternoon when we arrived at the chalet.

"So, what do you want to do?" he asked.

"Let's just walk on the beach," I said.

"I heard you did a great job at the clinics this week."

"It was quite rewarding seeing how well the clinics are running and how the community is responding to the services."

We took our shoes off and walked towards the ocean.

"I missed you," he said as he held my hands.

"Brahim, this is a mistake."

"The mistake was for us to think we could live without one another," he said caressing my face.

Slowly, he moved his hands to hold my chin and pulled my face gently towards his lips. After our lips touched, all the passion that flowed through our bodies just erupted. It was unavoidable. We fell to the sand and kept kissing. After a few minutes we walked back to the chalet and into the bedroom where we made love until we were exhausted. We didn't talk much. We just wanted to be in each others' arms. When the time approached, we headed out to see our Mediterranean sunset. It was more beautiful than I remembered. The bright tones of pink, orange, and yellow blending over a deep blue sky were a reminder of God's creation.

I had never felt so moved and blessed in my life. As that big, fiery orange sun disappeared, all my troubles seemed to melt away and I was truly happy if just for one last time.

The next morning, I took a taxi and left before Brahim woke up. I couldn't say goodbye. I wanted to stay, but I had to go. I didn't want to end it, but I didn't know how to keep it alive. On the way home, all I could think was of Brahim and what had probably been our last night together. I also remembered the legend of

Antarah and Ablah and wondered how they were able to endure so many obstacles yet beat the odds and in the end, make their love triumph over all.

When I got home, I took a nap. I was so tired of thinking. I woke up a few hours later and decided to take a shower. As I soaped my body, tears rolled down my cheeks and were swept away by the water. I thought of all the things I had always hoped for, and how twisted it had turned out. Suddenly, I felt a pair of hands roaming over my back. I jumped in fear.

"Afraid? It's just me darling. Your loving husband," Fouad said.

"Don't ever do that again," I said, irritated. "You could have at least called my name and let me know you were here."

"And spoil the surprise? Why are you so agitated anyway? I thought you'd be thrilled to see me after being apart for over four months."

"I'm sorry. You scared me and I overreacted."

He proceeded to take my sponge and soap my body.

"I missed every inch of your perfect body. Can you tell?"

"I missed you too."

"Come on baby, I want to make love to you."

"Now? Here?" I stuttered.

"You don't expect me to wait another four months, do you? Don't you want me as much as I want you?"

"Yes, of course."

There was no turning back. I was pinned against the marble. No way out. He made love to me roughly, the way he liked it. He performed with the desperation of a man who hadn't had sex in months, although I knew this wasn't the case. He had Esmaa.

Afterwards, he insisted on taking me to dinner.

"I want you to wear this," he said as he showed me a stunning dress he had bought for me.

"It's lovely, thank you."

As I was getting dressed, he came from behind and placed a necklace on my neck.

"Do you like it?" he asked

"Very much. You didn't have to bring me all of this."

"It's the least I could do for my beautiful wife."

"When you left, we weren't even on good terms."

"Time heals all wounds," he said. "I see you bought yourself some new bracelets. I'm a bit surprised considering I showered you with bracelets on our wedding day and you hardly ever wear them."

"The bracelets belonged to my mother. I brought them back with me from D.C." I nervously responded and held them as I remembered the day Brahim gave them to me at the chalet.

"Where's your mom's bracelet with the heart locket?"

"Well, you are very observant today. It's at the jewelers, the clasp broke."

"I see." He paused. "How was it? Being back in your father's house?"

"Okay, I guess."

"I regret not being with you during that time. Did you get everything settled with the attorney?"

"Yes."

"Ready to go? You look gorgeous."

I was surprised he didn't push for more information regarding my father's will.

We arrived to a very exclusive military V.I.P. restaurant.

"Our next house will be in this area," he said.

"I didn't know you were dissatisfied with your house," I said.

"Our house, dear, and I'm not. I just think my queen deserves the best and that's what I want to give her."

I wondered if he was referring to Esmaa.

"Can we afford this neighborhood?" I asked, trying to bait him into mentioning my inheritance.

He didn't answer.

The host walked us to our table and Fouad excused himself to make a phone call. I knew he was calling his lover, but I had to be certain. I followed him but I could not make out any part of the conversation, so I returned to the table while he spoke on the phone.

"So, what did you find out my beautiful spy?" Fouad asked.

"I know for a fact that your wife is sleeping with a Dr. Al-Kateb," Esmaa said. "I guess your perfect Fatima is no angel. I followed them to their love nest, a chalet on the beach. Isn't that romantic? They were there last night."

"That slut is going to pay dearly for her betrayal."

"Now that's the Fouad I know and love. Stay focused. You have twenty million reasons to smile. That should be enough to finance our operation."

"Meet me in my office in an hour. You've done a wonderful job and it calls for a celebration."

"I wouldn't miss it for the world."

Fouad returned to the table.

"Sorry, Fatima. Duty calls. I have to get back to the office. Stay and have dinner. I'll see you later tonight at home," he said, kissing my cheek.

Right after he left, I had a taxi follow him to his office and confirmed his meeting with Esmaa. Maybe I wanted to justify my own affair. But what I had with Brahim was more than sex; I had deep feelings for him. I was in love.

I wanted to go see Brahim so badly, but I couldn't face him. I felt that I had let him down because I couldn't avoid having sex with Fouad. So I went home to think over my future. A future that held two things certain: a loveless marriage and the loss of the only happiness I had ever known.

Fouad got home very late that night. The next morning, I woke up before him, got ready and went to work. I was hoping not to run into Brahim. I was going to try to avoid him.

Later that morning I had an unpleasant visitor.

"Good morning," Fouad said as he stepped into my office and closed the door. "No kiss for your loving husband?"

I gave him a quick peck on the lips.

"I wanted to apologize for last night. I thought you would wake me up to shower with you and have a repeat of yesterday's performance."

"I didn't want to wake you. I assumed you were very tired after traveling most of the day and then working late."

"You're so considerate."

Suddenly, the door opened.

"What happened to you yesterday?" Brahim raised his voice as he walked toward me.

I panicked.

Within seconds, he realized we weren't alone.

"Excuse the interruption. I should have knocked," Brahim apologized.

"That's quite alright, doctor," Fouad replied. "I take full responsibility if my wife missed a scheduled meeting yesterday, but we were making up for lost time."

"Fouad," I interrupted. "You remember Dr. Al-Kateb?"

They shook hands.

"Of course," he said. "I never forget my wife's associates."

"I truly forgot our appointment yesterday," I said. "I hope we can reschedule for later this week."

"That will be fine," Brahim said. "I'll leave you two alone. I'm sure you have a lot of catching up to do."

I could read the anger and disappointment in his eyes.

"Alone at last," Fouad said as he locked the door behind Brahim.

"What was that all about?" I said.

"What?"

"Making up for lost time…"

"Did I embarrass you?" he asked turning my body toward him.

"He's no stranger to you. Besides, I'm sure he knows I've been out for several months," he said as he attempted to kiss me and press against me. "He understands a man has needs."

"Fouad, this is a place of business not a bedroom," I said as I walked toward my chair wondering what was on Brahim's mind.

"I love it when you get serious. It's such a turn on," he said as he tried to sit me on the chair pushing his body over me.

"Stop it," I said, shoving him off.

He came close and kissed me, passionately biting my lips.

"I'll see you tonight at home. I expect you to finish what we started, or rather, didn't start here," he said.

I was relieved when he left. All I could think about was Brahim and what he was going through. I stared into the mirror for a few minutes. I tried to pull myself together before heading over to his office but he beat me to it.

"Brahim, I was just coming to see you," I said.

"Did you leave yesterday morning because you knew Fouad was coming home?"

"No, it was a total surprise. I didn't expect him for at least another month."

"So, are you okay? Did he hurt you in any way?" Brahim asked.

"No. I'm alright."

"I want to protect you from him, but how can I compete? I want you to be with me but he's your husband. I torture myself with the image of another man wanting every part of you; stroking your breasts, kissing your lips and every inch of your flawless body, caressing your hair, losing himself in your gorgeous, big, brown eyes," he said.

"I'm so sorry, but you have to know that I despise him and that my heart belongs only to you. I wish things were different. I wish I could have stopped this before it began to spare you the pain. I hope you believe me when I tell you that he means nothing to me and that you are the only man that I'll ever love."

"I believe you, habeebtee. But, it doesn't change the facts. Our hands are tied and there is no light at the end of this tunnel. I stand by my word; when you are ready to leave Fouad, I'll be here. I'll always protect you and will die for you," he said giving me a strong embrace. "I just want you to be safe. I don't want to lose you, but I'll sacrifice our love for your well-being."

I was speechless. Paralyzed. I knew all along my relationship with Brahim was doomed, but I had prayed for a miracle. Now, the man I loved was trying to hang on to any glimmer of hope and the man I loathed had come back to haunt me and destroy my happiness.

chapter 23

Rumors & Revelations

Weeks passed. Brahim and I ran into each other sporadically. Mostly, we just avoided each other. It hurt too much. I still looked at our picture, which I managed to keep well hidden, and fantasized about what could have been. When I had the house all to myself, I played my Sinatra tapes and remembered our getaways at the chalet and our sunsets. I often went to Jamila's just to sit on the balcony and catch a glimpse of that magical sunset. I hoped Brahim was somewhere looking at it too and thinking of me.

Fouad was spending more time at home and demanding more from me sexually. I wondered if his affair with Esmaa had fizzled. Unfortunately, I didn't love him anymore. He had my body, but my heart and soul were Brahim's, the man that changed my life forever.

Once a week, Fouad invited Rauf and some of his co-workers to play cards, smoke the bubble pipe, and drink coffee. He had become a bit of a homebody, making my life a little more unbearable.

My job had become very routine. Sometimes, I felt I had to drag myself out of bed. I had lost some of my enthusiasm. My biggest motivation for going to work these days was to avoid being around Fouad.

"There's a rumor circulating in the hospital," Dalal said.

"What is it?" I asked with curiosity.

"Dr. Brahim has been spotted several times with a woman," she paused when she saw my troubled expression. "What's wrong?"

"Nothing, I'm just surprised. Who is she? Does she work here?"

"All I know is that supposedly she's a knockout. I wouldn't expect anything less. He's a catch and he is so handsome."

"Well, good for him. He deserves to be happy. Keep me posted." I chuckled even though I was eaten up with jealousy.

When she left, I pounded my hands on the desk so hard that I thought I had broken a few fingers. I wanted to scream, confront him. But how could I.

My heart had just been torn to pieces. It was hard for me to believe that Brahim had moved on so quickly. Where was all that love he claimed to have for me? Then again, what could I expect? He knew he had no future with me. I had shattered his dreams. Why should I be shocked? He was probably doing the right thing. Still, I was emotionally devastated. His involvement with someone else made it so final. I wondered if he would take her to the chalet and share all our special places. Who was this lucky woman who was taking my place in Brahim's heart? Whoever she was, I was envious of her. Now I knew how he felt when he found out Fouad had returned to claim his place as my husband; empty, disgusted, frustrated, and defeated. I was sick to my stomach. I rushed to the bathroom and started throwing up.

The next two days I was off. I was still feeling sick. It was probably psychological. I laid in bed most of the first day. On the second day, I called the hospital disguising my voice. I asked to speak to Brahim. I had to find out if he was off. He was. I couldn't resist the crazy idea of going to the chalet to torment myself with the possibility that he might be there with his new love. I took a taxi to our getaway and it confirmed my darkest fear. There were two cars parked by the house. I nearly fainted. I rushed back home and threw myself in bed till the next morning. Fortunately, Fouad had been too busy to notice my strange behavior. He was probably working on his next conquest.

As I was getting ready to go to work the following morning, Fouad started getting frisky. I was definitely not in the mood.

"Why haven't you given me a son?" Fouad asked out of the blue.

"You should ask God that question."

"Why don't we start working on it right now?"

"I have to be at work in less than an hour."

"It shouldn't take long," he said as he tried to unzip my dress.

"I said not now."

"You've been rejecting me quite frequently. Work is starting to affect our home life."

"Please, Fouad. We've been together almost every night this week. Isn't that enough?"

"I could never get enough of you. Are you on any kind of birth control?"

"Where did that come from?"

"You're not answering my question."

"No. I'm not avoiding a pregnancy. I guess it just hasn't happened."

"I want you to go see a doctor and check out what's wrong with you."

"Oh, so now something is wrong with me. There's not a slight chance that you're the one with the problem."

"I doubt it."

"Why? Have you fathered any children I should know of?"

"Fatima, I don't like where this is heading. Just please your husband and go see a doctor."

"I'm leaving."

The man just infuriated me. I knew what the problem was. I had been using the pill without his knowledge. I could not imagine bringing a child into this farce of a marriage.

My days at the hospital went by slowly. All I could think about was Brahim and the woman in his life.

In a desperate attempt to find out if all the rumors were true, I went to his office. He wasn't there but there was a card on his desk addressed "Brahim." I couldn't resist the temptation, so I opened it.

"Thanks for the insatiable passion that we shared at the chalet. It was unforgettable. I await your call for a repeat performance." It was signed "E".

I thought of every possible female name that started with "E" and kept wondering who this woman could be. Then I heard noises, so I stuffed the card in my pocket. I probably shouldn't have done it; there was no need to keep tormenting myself. I had to move on, but how could I? I was losing the man that I loved.

As I rushed out of his office, he walked in and grabbed me by the arm.

"Fatme."

"Let me go," I said, as I shook his arm off mine.

I was hurt, and it was inevitable running into him. We worked at the same hospital and we were involved in the same projects. It probably would have been easier to give up my job. Fouad would definitely have approved. But I wasn't a quitter; I had earned the respect of my co- workers and was making a difference. So I decided to get even. I had to pick myself up and make Brahim believe my life was better off without him.

From that day on, I started looking my best, wearing everything I knew he loved on me, from my high heels to my perfume. I was ready to make him remember what he was missing. I went from making myself invisible to letting him know I was there. I hoped it was me he thought about every time he made love to her. Rumors kept swirling about Brahim and this mystery woman; this was the fuel that energized my every move.

Over the next two weeks, I grew strong and confident again. As I was walking into the hospital cafeteria, I heard a woman's voice calling my name.

"Fatima, how have you been?"

"Hi, Esmaa. What are you doing at the hospital?" I asked.

"Just waiting for my fiancee to come out of surgery."

"I didn't know you were seeing someone," besides my husband, I told myself, "let alone engaged."

This explained why Fouad might not have been seeing her.

"What happened to all that talk about work before family?" I asked sarcastically.

"I guess you were right. The man of my dreams came along, and I just couldn't resist."

"What's his name?"

"You know him. You guys worked together in that project with the clinics…"

"Dr. Al-Kateb?" I interrupted in disbelief.

"Brahim" she said.

I couldn't let my face give away my feelings for him. The "E" was for Esmaa. Brahim was going to marry my husband's former lover, of all people. This couldn't be happening. It was a cruel joke.

"I'm late for an appointment. We'll catch up later," I said storming out of the cafeteria.

I was devastated and disillusioned. There was no turning back the clock. There was no more future for Brahim and I. He had made his choice, but I had to see him one more time. Ironically, I was wearing the same dress I had on the first time we kissed.

"Don't read anything into me being here," I said. "I just came to give these back."

I painfully took off the three bracelets he had given me. I needed to make a clean break.

"What's this all about?' Brahim asked.

"Do you have to ask?" I said agitated. "It's over."

"Calm down, Fatme."

"Don't ask me to calm down. How could you do this to me with her of all people? Are there not enough women out there that you have to settle for Fouad's scraps? You make me sick. How did I ever believe in you? God! How could I have been so wrong about you?"

"What are you talking about?" he said, grabbing me and pulling me close.

"Don't touch me. You disgust me."

At that point, Brahim pulled me close and gave me the steamiest kiss we had ever shared. It was a mixture of love, hate, lust, and hurt. I tried to break away but I was consumed by the moment. I wanted time to come to a halt. Finally, I pushed him away and slapped him.

"That's the last time that will ever happen," I said slamming his door.

As I walked down the hallway, I ran into Esmaa. "Your fiance is out

from surgery," I told her in a snappy voice and kept walking.

I went straight to my office and locked the door. I stayed in there for hours, mostly crying and feeling sorry for myself. I felt so weak and alone. I could still feel Brahim's touch. His scent was on my body. I wanted to shake off all these feelings, but I kept thinking about that last kiss. There was a knock on the door.

"Fatima, are you alright?" Dalal asked.

"Hold on," I wiped my tears and put on a smile as I opened the door.

"You look pale," she said.

"I haven't been feeling well for the past couple of days. My stomach has been upset."

"Is Fouad stressing you out?"

"Doesn't he always? His latest obsession is that he wants a son."

"You're not pregnant, are you?"

"No way. I've been taking precautions. A baby is the last thing on my mind these days."

"You might find motherhood very rewarding."

"If I had the right man by my side, maybe."

"Have you been crying?"

"You know what, I'm exhausted. I think I'll be heading home. Thanks for checking up on me, Dalal. You're a good friend."

As I started to walk, I fainted. When I woke up, I was in a hospital room with an IV in my arm and Dalal by my side.

"Well, good evening sleepy head."

"Where am I? What happened to me?"

"I guess God heard Fouad's prayers," Dalal said.

"What do you mean?"

"You're pregnant."

"That's impossible. Where's the doctor?" I asked frantically. "I need to talk to him. Fouad can't know about this. Please tell me you haven't told anyone."

"No, relax. Dr. Hazem did the examination and I personally worked on your blood work"

"Have you called Fouad?"

"I left him a message to contact me regarding his wife."

"Dalal, call the doctor now. Please."

The door opened.

"Dr. Hazem, I was just going to look for you."

"Doctor, I need your complete discretion in this matter," I interrupted. "No one should know I'm expecting not even my husband."

"I respect your wishes but you are already two and a half months into your pregnancy, and pretty soon you won't be able to conceal it."

"Thanks, doctor. I'll take your advice into consideration. Just promise me you won't tell anyone about my condition."

"You have my word," the doctor said. He then exited the room.

"Fatima, this baby is Fouad's, isn't it?"

"Dalal, this conversation cannot leave this room," I said weeping.

"You can trust me. Talk to me."

"This can't be Fouad's child. The father of my baby is a man I love with all my heart. I can't believe this is happening, not now. I'm so confused. I don't know what to do."

"Who's the father?"

"I can't tell you his name. I can't put you in any danger. The less you know, the better off you'll be. If Fouad found out, there would be hell to pay."

"What are you going to do? You're running out of time."

"I need to think very carefully. When Fouad calls you back, tell him I had to go help out at one of the clinics out of town, some kind of emergency, and that I might have to spend the night. This will give me some time alone to clear my mind. I know I should be happy. I know this is a blessing from God, but the timing is all wrong. I don't want anyone to know I'm here, especially Dr. Brahim."

"Dr. Brahim? Oh no! He's…"

"Dalal, just go make sure Fouad gets the message before he comes looking for me."

"I'll do that right now."

I cried. I cried tears of sorrow, but mostly tears of joy. God had brought a ray of sunshine into my otherwise pathetic life. This was the most beautiful gift I could imagine. This baby was the product of a love so deep and pure that I had no choice but to embrace it. All I could do was think about Brahim. I had hoped things between us would have turned out differently. I wished I could share this incredible news with him and his family. If we had only run into the sunset when we had the chance, today we'd be sharing the happiest day of our lives. I was a coward. Brahim was willing to take a chance on me, but my fear of Fouad drove us apart. Now, I had a tough decision to make; a decision that would affect not only me, but my unborn child as well. What was I to do? Fouad desperately wanted an offspring and Brahim had moved on with his life. At this point, the obvious choice was to have Fouad believe the baby was his. But I needed more time to make that decision.

Dalal stayed by my side most of the evening.

"Talk to me," she said.

"There's nothing to say. The man I love, the father of my child is getting married."

"What? How long has he known this woman?"

"That's not the worst part. I found out who she is."

"Who? Do I know her?"

"All too well. It's Esmaa."

"No way. That snake! There is no way Dr. Brahim fell for her."

"Oh, but he did. I won't deny she is very attractive and ambitious. I'm sure he is drawn to her but, marriage? How could he?" I asked while tears rolled down my cheeks.

"I still can't believe it."

"She told me herself and I found a card on his desk that confirmed their involvement."

"Did you ask him?"

"Not in so many words."

"So, you don't know for certain."

"Why would she lie? What would she gain? She doesn't know about us."

"You have a point but still I thought Dr. Brahim was smarter than that."

"Well, he was on the rebound and I guess people do stupid things when they feel betrayed. We had talked about leaving together before Fouad came back but I was afraid of the repercussions. Then, my husband surprised me by showing up unexpectedly and Brahim walked in on us at the office. Fouad insinuated to Brahim that we had been intimate the night before. From that moment, we distanced ourselves."

"Does Jamila or anyone else know?"

"No, and it has to stay that way. I can't deny that it feels good to finally have someone to talk to, but the situation is too delicate to involve more people."

"How are things between you and Fouad?"

"The same. He's been spending more time at home, but I can't trust him anymore. He has been unfaithful so many times that I've lost my trust in him. Now my heart belongs to someone else, and God has blessed me with his child. I will never be able to love Fouad. I might stay with him till death due us part, but he'll never take Brahim's place."

"A relationship with Dr. Brahim is a dead end. My advice to you is to forget about him and move on with Fouad. Maybe the baby will bring you together and will make Fouad devote himself to his family."

"How could I forget Brahim when I'm going to have a constant reminder of our love?"

"You'll have to try, one day at a time. Time will heal your broken heart. You might consider taking a leave of absence, putting some distance between the both of you."

"I'll think about that. It's probably the best thing I could do."

"Get some rest now. You have to take care of that little one. I'll be back in the morning."

I managed to sleep a few hours. I had so much on my mind. Dalal was in my room bright and early.

"Fouad called. I told him you'd be home by noon. I thought I would buy you a little more time."

"Thanks but I'd rather go home. Hopefully he will be at work and I can relax till the evening."

"Good luck, my friend. Call me if you need anything."

I headed home, hoping not to see Fouad. It was too early for a confrontation. I noticed a car close to the house. It reminded me of the car I had seen by the chalet. I walked in quietly and overheard voices. It was Samira's day off so I knew Fouad had to be talking to someone else.

"You're sure she didn't spend the night with her lover?" Fouad said.

"Not a chance. She probably went somewhere to lick her wounds. You should have seen her face when I told her that Dr.

Brahim and I were engaged. It was like a rug had been pulled out from under her."

"Good. The whore deserves to suffer."

"I must say it was a perfect plan. It just took paying off a few nurses to spread the word, then parking the car at the chalet a couple of evenings. That lusty card on his desk was a stroke of genius, and to top it all off, our accidental meeting at the hospital where I brought up the wedding. It was all brilliant, if I do say so myself."

"You were brilliant as usual," Fouad said as he kissed her. "That's what I love about you: Machiavellian brains and a body that no man would be able to resist."

"Thank you, I'm flattered. How about we put this body to work?"

"Bastards!" I said to myself.

I had heard more than enough. I silently exited the house and left them to do what I knew they did best. They were truly perfect for each other. In some ways, I felt like the weight of the world had been lifted off my shoulders. I was elated that Brahim was true to me, that our last kiss was as real as it felt. He loved me as much as I loved him. The problem was that Fouad knew about our relationship and I suspected this little plot was just the beginning of a much more elaborate plan to destroy us.

I wondered how they found out. Obviously, Esmaa was instrumental in the orchestration of this set up. Now I understood why Fouad had come home all of a sudden and had made a point to let Brahim know that our marriage was back on track. Unfortunately, I knew it would take more than staging a relationship between Brahim and Esmaa for Fouad to avenge his injured ego.

This unexpected discovery made my options clear. It was impossible for this monster to rear my child. Fouad would have serious doubts about his paternity. Therefore, it was imperative that he not learn about my pregnancy. He was more than capable of trying to harm the baby. This made me feel trapped. I needed time to come up with a plan.

chapter 24

Death & Suspicion

It was Thursday evening, the day of Fouad's weekly gathering at the house with the guys. I was surprised that he had given Samira the day off.

I arrived home a little late, hoping the men were there and I could avoid an argument. I doubted he would make a scene in front of his friends. Besides, I was sure that he was still gloating about his successful scheme, so he probably wouldn't bother harassing me.

I entered the house, quietly hoping to go undetected. I heard a voice in the study and was reassured to know someone was with him. As I got closer to see who it was, I realized he was on the phone and decided to eavesdrop on his conversation.

"We are doing this tonight. I'll keep him here a little longer than usual and call you when he leaves."

Now that we were alone, I knew I'd have to to make my presence known. I headed back towards the main door and began to rattle my keys. As I walked past the study, Fouad stopped me.

"Where do you think you're going?"

"Fouad, this again? Didn't Dalal call you and explain the emergency?"

"Yes. Still, I was expecting you home much earlier especially because your behavior was unacceptable. Do you remember what happened the last time you didn't sleep at home?"

"Yes, and I hope there won't be a repeat performance. I'm sorry. It all happened so fast, and I knew Dalal had spoken to you..."

"I was gone for four months and a clinic is more important than me," he said in anger, ready to strike.

This was going to be another way to release his wrath because of my betrayal. Luckily, the bell rang. I rushed to open the door. It was Rauf.

"Hi brother," Fouad said, composing himself.

"Let me help you with those bags," I told Rauf as we headed to the kitchen.

"I thought we'd give Samira a break today and try some food from this Greek restaurant that just opened in the city."

"That was very thoughtful, Rauf," I said.

Fouad headed to the study to look for some papers he wanted to show Rauf. The phone rang and I could hear Fouad in the background.

"I really appreciate you not telling Fouad that you ran into me in D.C."

"I truly want to apologize for that night. It wasn't my finest hour. I hope you've forgiven me," he said.

"It's all forgotten. You've been very kind to me. I consider you a friend."

"I got those reports you wanted to see," Fouad shouted from the study for Rauf to join him.

I stayed in the kitchen setting everything up for the rest of the guests. The voices from the study kept getting louder as if Fouad and Rauf were arguing, but I couldn't make out what they were saying. Minutes later Fouad came to the kitchen.

"Is everything Ok?" I asked.

"I want you upstairs right now."

"What about the food?"

"I'll take care of it. Our conversation is not over. I'll deal with you after my guests leave."

As I headed upstairs, Rauf asked, "Are you going to be joining us?"

"No, I'm a bit tired. I nibbled on some food while I was heating it up. It's delicious, thank you. I'll be upstairs if you need me," I said turning to Fouad.

I stayed in my room most of the evening, but I managed to go downstairs and listen in on another mysterious conversation. The guys were sipping Scotch, smoking Cuban cigars, and playing cards but Fouad was M.I.A.

Quietly, I went down the hall and heard Fouad's voice coming from the guest bedroom. He was on the phone and the door was ajar.

"They're all still here. Be patient, just a little longer. After tonight, we'll be closer than we've ever been to our goal. Tonight will mark the beginning of our reign."

Something was definitely going on, but what? I returned to the bedroom and managed to fall asleep until I was awaken by lightning at 1:30 am. It was storming. I heard Fouad speaking to Rauf. I was surprised he was still here. Fouad was insisting that he spend the night. He was concerned because the mountain roads were dark and had many sharp turns. Rauf was very stubborn and insisted on leaving.

Right after he left, Fouad was on the phone. It was becoming obvious the earlier conversations had to do with Rauf. I went back to bed and pretended to be asleep although my head kept spinning trying to figure out what this all meant.

At 3:45 AM., the phone rang. Fouad started to pace up and down as he spoke. He progressively got more and more emotional. He hung up and started getting dressed.

"What happened?" I asked.

"It's Rauf."

"What about Rauf?"

"He's dead," Fouad said in tears. "He was driving and talking on the phone with Abdul. When they abruptly got disconnected, Abdul and a few other bodyguards decided to head towards our house to make sure Rauf was alright. As they drove up the hill, they saw his Ferrari up in flames."

"But how? Did he leave our house drunk? Please tell me you didn't let him drive drunk."

"Of course not. I even asked him to spend the night because of the bad weather. You know Rauf. He's hard headed. Apparently his car went off the road and exploded on impact. His body was burned beyond recognition."

"Are they sure it was Rauf?"

"Yes, the platinum ring he wore was still on his finger. It was his favorite ever since college. His mother gave it to him as a gift on his twentieth birthday. It was engraved with his initials," Fouad said, breaking down in tears. "I should have hidden his keys and not let him out of this house."

Fouad appeared to be very distraught with the news, almost vulnerable. I actually felt sorry for him. I was devastated by this news. Rauf was a good man. So young, so full of life; it was truly a tragedy.

"It's not your fault. Where are you going?" I asked as he grabbed his car keys.

"I have to be there when the President arrives. He'll need my support."

"I'll go with you."

"Not now, Fatima. I need to do this alone."

As I walked Fouad to the door, I sensed the tension. He was nervous and stressed out. This was unusual for a man who always kept his composure through tense situations. His best friend had just died but my gut told me something wasn't right.

"Be careful out there. Please give the president and his family my condolences."

With Fouad gone, I let all my emotions overflow and started to cry inconsolably. Now that I was getting ready to be a mother, I could start to understand what Rauf's parents had to be going through. I really felt for President Saeed and his wife. They had lost their only son. The young man they had groomed from childhood to take over the presidency one day, so many hopes, dreams, and expectations had come to a meaningless end without a warning. I could only imagine his mother's anguish. Her first-born child was dead at age thirty-two with so much to live for. Outliving a child had to be an unbearable pain. I wondered if their faith was strong enough to pull them through this. Only God had the answers to all my questions. I had to believe there was a divine reason for all of this to happen yet it was so difficult to make sense of his loss.

Sleep was out of the question, so I went to the kitchen to make a cup of baboonesh. I hoped the chamomile tea would soothe my nerves. As I opened the cupboard and pulled out the box of tea, a small, plastic bottle fell on to the floor. When I picked it up, I realized it was a bottle of eye drops. As I wondered what the drops were doing in the kitchen, I got a chill up my spine and a strong feeling that something was wrong. The mysterious conversations, Fouad, Rauf… I followed my instincts and proceeded to put some drops of the substance on a swab to take to the lab for testing. Afterwards, I placed the bottle back where I found it.

Fouad hadn't made it back home. At sunrise, I took the sample to the hospital lab. They were very backed up so, I couldn't get the results immediately. I was terrified to confirm my suspicions, that my husband, a man that I had once imagined a future with, was a murderer.

Later that day, I met Fouad at the Presidential Palace. There was a private intimate ceremony for those closest to Rauf. I walked up to a distraught President Saeed and a pale, weak first lady to express my deep sorrow for their loss. The mood was so grim. His mother nearly fainted a couple of times. His sisters were by their parents' side giving them strength. Fouad stood behind the president and his wife like a son. He held Mrs. Saeed's hand as a sign of solidarity in her darkest hour.

The whole country was in mourning. President Saeed was beloved by most. He wasn't perfect, but he had done good and made a difference for his people. Everyone had expected for Rauf to rule the nation one day. Now, with his death and no brothers to fill his shoes, there was an air of uncertainty. All Antarah took to the streets to pay their last respects to Rauf and to offer support to the presidential family.

The roads were barricaded by military vehicles. A motorcade escorted the vehicle that carried the body all over the capital city. All throughout the country, people showed their compassion for a life taken too soon. Fouad rode with the president and his entourage. I followed in a separate car with his mother and sisters. As we rode all over town, the people held up handwritten poster boards with pictures of Rauf and slogans: "God Bless Our Hero," "Our souls and our blood for our Hero," "A Palace in Heaven awaits for you, our Hero." Rauf's mother was extremely emotional as she observed how an entire nation had united in memory of her son. All their personal grief had turned public.

While the women waited outside the cemetery, I saw a small hill with a shrine built to lay the body to rest and to accommodate the men to pray for his eternal life. Everything was so grandiose. It was, after all, the president's only son. The moment was sad. Seeing the oversized pictures of Rauf made me go back to the day when I first met him. He was such a charming and charismatic individual. He probably would have made a good president, and I'm sure a good husband and father with the right woman by his side.

When the men came out, I saw Brahim. Immediately, Fouad came by my side and wrapped his arms around me. This whole experience reminded me that life was too short, and that I had wasted too much time being unhappy.

Fouad sent me home while he accompanied the president.

There, I cried for a while thinking about my parents. I spoke to them and told them they would soon be grandparents. I would have given anything to have them before me and see their joyous reaction to my news. Unfortunately, I was all alone. It had been a long, depressing day.

A few days later, I got a call from the lab. They had found traces of diazepam, better known as valium, on the swab. I had an eerie feeling. There weren't many people I could trust, but I knew I could count on Brahim. He was in surgery, so I waited patiently in his office. Finally, he came in.

"I know we haven't been speaking, and I know I was wrong to slap you, but I need your help," I said. "Tell me everything you know about a drug called diazepam."

"Slow down. What's this all about?"

"Please Brahim, just tell me."

"Diazepam is used to relieve anxiety, insomnia, and nervousness, as well as certain types of seizures and muscle spasms. In the States, most people know it as Valium, and you require a prescription for it because it's highly addictive. In this country, on the other hand, it's readily available over the counter," Brahim said.

"What are the side effects of an overdose?"

"You're scaring me Fatima. Did you…?"

"No, just answer my question."

"Sleepiness, drowsiness, dizziness, hallucinations, severe confusion; the person might appear drunk or unconscious. Fatima, does this have anything to do with Rauf's death?" Brahim asked.

"Thanks, Brahim. I can't talk about it right now."

My worst fear was confirmed. Something had bothered me from the beginning about Rauf's death. He was an avid car racer. Although he loved speed, he was a very safe driver and he knew that road like the palm of his hand. He wasn't one to take unnecessary risks. He knew his father was depending on him to take over the leadership of the country. He took that responsibility very seriously. I know he wouldn't have done anything foolish.

I was scared. If Fouad was capable of murder, my life was in jeopardy.

"Fatima, wait," Brahim said as he followed me to my office.

"Lock the door," I said frantically. "Fouad knows about us. I think he killed Rauf and we could be next on his hit list."

"Slow down. What do you mean he knows about us? Did you tell him?"

"No. Apparently he had us followed by his lover. She paid off some people to spread rumors about the both of you being engaged…"

"Why didn't you just ask me and we could have cleared this up?"

"It was easier to slap you. I was crazed, enraged with jealousy. I wasn't thinking straight. I'm sorry. Now, I'm terrified. There is no telling what he can do."

Brahim held me tight in his arms.

"I love you and I swear I won't let that bastard harm you. I promised you once that I would take care of you and that's what I intend to do. Regrettably, all we have is speculation. We need to find concrete evidence to link him to this crime."

"Greed, power, those are the motives. Fouad is second in command to the most powerful position after the presidency. Rauf's death left the door wide open for Fouad to slide in and take his place, not only as the head of the Republican Guard, but also, as a son to a president that needs to fill a void. Fouad has worked hard throughout the years to earn the president's trust and he is considered part of their family.

I think he sees the president as a surrogate father because he lost his dad at a young age. Yet, Fouad knew he would always play second fiddle to Rauf. The only way he could achieve his goal was murder. That night Rauf was at our house. I'm sure Fouad laced his drink to guarantee he'd fall asleep behind the wheel and lose control of the vehicle. It makes perfect sense."

"I guess it's very possible. How about an accomplice?"

"Maybe Esmaa, his lover. She seems to share his passion for deceit. I don't know. All I know is that we have to be very careful. We can't be seen together. Fouad is under the impression that I broke it off for good. I need you now more than ever."

We just hugged each other tight.

"I want to be with you so bad it hurts," Brahim said.

"Me too, but we'll have to wait for the right time."

Spy Games

The next steps I took were aimed at uncovering Fouad's involvement in Rauf's death. I decided to plant a voice- activated recorder in his study, hoping to tape an incriminating conversation. While Fouad spent time with the president, trying to secure Rauf's position, I snooped around and planted my own traps.

"What's so important? Am I looking at the new head of the Republican Guard? Oh, no. What the hell happened? I thought it was a sure thing," Esmaa said.

"So did I," a furious Fouad replied as the sound of things crashing was heard. "That old son of a bitch. I've been like a son to him, and this is how he repays me."

"So who did that bastard appoint to your position?"

"His brother."

"His brother! His brother is a loser; the biggest asshole in town. He has as much military experience as I have in brain surgery. His notoriety consists in seducing women and making fast money. The only reason he's gotten this far is because of his last name. This is fucking unbelievable. I guess blood is thicker than water after all."

At that moment, a piece of glass was thrown against a surface.

"Saeed and his family are going to pay dearly for this."

"I'm sure they will. You just have to say the word, my darling. All our key players are in position awaiting your instructions. We are ready at any time. "

"Patience, dear Esmaa. Soon, very soon, President Saeed will regret ever meeting me. I swear on my father's grave," he said slamming his fist on the desk.

I had listened to the first in a series of tapes that would help me build the necessary evidence to bury my husband. Still, I needed more tangible proof if I wanted to expose him and his lover. Lately, Fouad was in a foul mood. He couldn't get over not being promoted. Even his appetite for sex had diminished. I wasn't complaining. Every evening, he locked himself in his study for hours, probably plotting his next move. I hoped he'd bring home files that might uncover his future plans. For days, I looked in his study for any valuable information unsuccessfully. The following day, I went to his office. I knew he wouldn't be there because I overheard him scheduling a lunch meeting.

"Good afternoon, Mrs. Aziz. It's been a while since you've come by the office," his secretary said.

"Hello Leila, I came to take my husband to lunch," I said.

"The Major General is not in. He had a meeting."

"Will he be long?"

"I really don't know."

"I'll wait in his office for a few minutes. Hopefully he'll be back shortly."

I entered Fouad's office and closed the door. I could smell Esmaa.

The scent of vanilla and sandalwood had become synonymous with repulsive.

Having no time to waste, I started looking in his drawers, file cabinets, anywhere I felt might hold the answers. Behind a small table, I found a safe box. I reached over and realized I needed a key. I went back to his desk to retrieve a series of keys hoping one would open the box. As I was ready to start trying the keys, I saw the door handle turn. I put the keys in my pocket. A woman entered.

"Fatima, what are you doing in Fouad's office?" Esmaa asked.

"I'm his wife. Remember?" I said.

"I didn't mean it that way. I'm just surprised to see you here."

"Fouad has been working so hard lately, I wanted to take his mind off things. You know what I mean. Now, if you'll excuse me, I have to get ready for my husband."

I could see the jealous rage in her eyes. It felt good to make her green with envy. She knew I was a formidable opponent and that Fouad wouldn't resist me. This was just the beginning of my payback for all the betrayal that had kept me from my happiness. By now, I felt I had wasted too much time and it was too risky to attempt opening the safe. I quickly put the keys back and looked forward to another opportunity.

"I heard you came looking for me today," Fouad said when he got home.

"Who told you? Esmaa?" I said. "She's extremely protective of you."

"That's Esmaa's way. So, what were you doing in my office?"

"I thought we could have lunch. Lately, we've barely spent any time together."

"You've missed me?"

"Is that so hard to believe?"

"Let me take you to dinner."

"That would be nice."

I had no choice but to go along. At the restaurant, I complained about feeling ill to avoid any intimacy that evening. Fortunately, it worked. The next morning, he had an early start. He was going out of town for the day. I made him breakfast in bed and massaged his feet. I tried to distract him promising an unforgettable night of passion. It worked. He was running so late, he left without his briefcase. I hoped my visit to his office had prompted him to bring home something of interest. I rushed to the study and went through his briefcase. I found what I was looking for. It was a bombshell. Fouad had been keeping a detailed journal since his teenage years. It was odd that a man like him would express his emotions on paper. I anticipated unraveling many secrets. First and foremost, why did he marry me? And last, but definitely not least, why did he murder Rauf?

As I turned the pages, I found, tucked between two pages, a yellowish envelope containing a letter. I immediately opened it, hoping it would be a key to the past.

My dearest Fouad:

If you are reading this letter, it's because I'm dead. Just know that I loved you and your sisters very much. You are now the man of the house and I expect you to take this task very seriously.

The man responsible for my death is General Gaffar Abdul Aziz, the head of the military police and an associate of mine. His position is among the most powerful in the country. He can make people disappear without a trace and make anything happen. He controls the borders and its patrols.

I am his middle man. I arrange the transport of over 500 kilos of hashish in eighteen-wheelers coming from Jordan to Antarah. The General makes sure these trucks cross the border without a hitch.

We have done many of these operations and I have made him a very rich man. This last time was supposed to be no different, but there was an accident. Another truck hit our truck on the back, and it overturned, breaking the lining carrying the drugs. There was hashish everywhere.

There were witnesses to the event so, a full report had to be filed by the book. This was a situation the General could not control.

The driver was questioned and a proper investigation took place. Everything was kept out of the media. Everyone involved was intimidated into never speaking about the incident.

Unfortunately, someone will have to take the fall and that will probably be me. I'd rather kill myself than go to prison and put my family through shame.

It is your duty to use this information wisely and make him pay for his betrayal. I know you will make me proud.

Your father,

Hussein Mustafa

I couldn't believe what I had just read. A range of emotions, from anger to contempt, invaded my being. It was hard to believe that my father had set in motion this destructive chain of events. I finally understood what I overheard Fouad tell Esmaa about settling a score. I had only been a pawn in their game. I asked myself how my father could have sacrificed me, his only daughter, to save his skin. I was devastated by what I had just learned. Suddenly, I heard a car door close. Instinctively, I put the letter back in the journal and into his briefcase. I dried my tears and collected myself before anyone came in. I walked out of the study just in time.

"What are you doing back so soon? I thought you were headed out of town," I said.

"Where's my briefcase?" Fouad asked in a serious tone.

"I assumed it was with you,"

"Would I be here if that were the case?"

"Are you implying that I purposely hid it from you?"

"I wouldn't put it past you," he paused. "It must be in the study. Damn it, I can't afford this kind of distractions before an exercise."

"It's a no win situation with you."

"I need to go. I don't have time for this."

I walked him to the door and slammed it. He couldn't leave soon enough. I was so angry I just wanted to scream. I hated Fouad; I loathed my father. This man had been the center of my universe all my life. He was my hero, my role model. Now, his image was crushed forever. I felt I never knew this man I called Baba.

I had to wonder if my mother was aware of my father's other life, and if she would have supported his decision to marry me off to my tormenter. I thought of all the money he left me; drug money, dishonest money, money that resulted in pain, death, and misery for many people, including Fouad.

Maybe Fouad had the right to be angry and use me the way he did. After all, General Aziz had taken away his father and his chance at a normal life. Fouad was a product of his environment; of a hatred that ran so deep it had turned him into a monster. He was incapable of loving anyone, not even himself.

Rauf had probably been a target all along. Fouad was resentful of Rauf's good fortune and hoped to slip into his life after eliminating him. When his plan backfired, he decided to go after the President, a man whom he also held responsible, on some level, for his father's death.

I was so depressed. I needed Brahim so much. I went to the hospital hoping to talk to him. He was off, so I took a chance and went to the chalet. His car was there.

"Fatima, I can't believe you're here," Brahim said as he hugged me tight.

"I know I told you we had to keep our distance, but I had to come. I needed to feel your arms around me. I needed someone to talk to. I don't know where to begin…"

I told Brahim about the taped conversations and Fouad's journal. He was shocked to learn all the sordid details.

"I'm so sorry, Fatima. I know how much you loved your father. But people make mistakes."

"Not the kind of mistakes that destroy other people's lives. Not the kind of mistakes that turn someone into a murderer."

"Fouad made his own choices."

"Still, if Fouad's father were alive, he might have turned out differently."

"We will never know. So, what now? Fatima, you are in a very delicate situation."

"I know, but I still don't have enough evidence to put Fouad away. These are some serious allegations. Without concrete proof, I am really digging my own grave. Fouad could always turn the tables and make it seem as if I am the mastermind of his plot."

"How can I help you?"

"You are. Just listening to me and being here for me gives me the strength and courage I need to conquer my fears."

"I don't want you to be afraid. I just want you to be free of all your past, of all this pain that is eating up your soul."

"Brahim, make love to me. Make love to me as if it's the last time our bodies will become one. Make me forget all this ugliness in my life. Make me happy if only for one last time."

Slowly and gently, he undressed me. He kissed every single corner of my body, caressed my skin with the tenderness of our first time. He stroked every part of me into deep relaxation and kissed me deeply and intensely. He licked my breasts with the tip of his tongue, giving my whole being a delightful sensation. I anticipated the moment that he had carefully built for my pleasure.

Finally, our bodies came together. It was a heavenly experience that fulfilled both of us, bringing smiles to our faces. At that point, I wanted to tell him about our baby. I knew this news would bring such joy to his life. But, I couldn't. I had to follow through with my plans and make a clean cut with Fouad if I ever had a chance for happiness. I needed Brahim safe from Fouad's poisonous claws.

"I've never felt closer to you than at this moment," he said.

"You make me forget all my sadness with all your love. Brahim, I love you more than ever. I know we'll be together soon, I feel it. Just a little longer…"

"I love you, habeebtee. My life is worthless without you. I will wait as long as it takes to be with you. I just need you to be careful and to know you can count on me for anything."

It was getting close to nightfall. We both walked hand in hand towards our Mediterranean sunset, wondering if this would be our last.

"I have to go. Thanks for making me happy," I said as I kissed him goodbye.

On my way home, I thought of Brahim. He was the calm before the storm; he gave me strength. He was the love of my life, my rock, my reason to live. Now I was carrying a child, our child, a ray of light at the end of a long, dark tunnel.

chapter 26

Lives In Jeopardy & Secrets Revealed

When I arrived to the house, reality set in. As I opened the door, Esmaa walked out.

"Since when do you make house calls?" I asked.

"I've been waiting for you."

"For me? What do you want?"

"Some advice on men. On one man in particular, Brahim," Esmaa said.

"Trouble in paradise already? Maybe you should forget about doctors and stick to military personnel. I think they suit your personality much better. Besides, I'm beat. We'll have to catch up some other time," I said as I walked up the stairs to my room.

I was actually glad to know Esmaa and Fouad were together. This meant that I might have some new, recorded conversations that would give me some needed ammunition to bring them down.

"Why didn't you come see me in the study?" Fouad asked.

"You were busy with Esmaa," I replied.

"Esmaa was bringing me some papers I left at the office."

"That's not what she told me."

"Can we stop talking about her and talk about this morning?"

"What about it?"

"I know I was a little harsh. I needed to be in the field conducting some weapons tests. I was already running late and then, I had to come back to get some important data I had left in my briefcase. It was just one of those days and I unfairly took it out on you."

"And now you want to kiss and make up, and you want me to live up to the promises I made to you this morning. Well, I hate to disappoint you, but I'm tired and I want to go to bed. Next time treat me with respect."

I was very firm. I couldn't make love to him after everything I had uncovered and after being with Brahim. I hoped he would accept what I told him and let me be. He went back to his study. The next day, he woke up very early and left with his briefcase in hand. I saw him from the window. I looked forward to last night's recorded conversation.

"Esmaa, What are you doing here? I told you not to come by the house anymore."

"I had to know if tonight was the night."

"I can't do it. At least not tonight," Fouad said.

"You're in love with that bitch aren't you? Are you ever going to kill her or will I have to do it myself?"

"Esmaa, I give the orders. She will die when I say it's time."

"Without her twenty million, we have no future."

"You think I don't know that? Soon, we'll have it all. In a matter of days, Antarah will be ours. Together we will be indestructible."

"So, what are you waiting for? Why haven't you eliminated your sweet Fatima?"

"I know what I'm doing. Timing is everything. Have you planted the evidence?"

"Of course. There will be no doubt that the good doctor murdered his lover in a jealous rage. Have you gotten rid of the diazepam you used on Rauf?"

"This house is free of anything that could incriminate me. Thanks for thinking of everything. That's why I love you."

"With Fatima dead and the doctor in jail, you will have fulfilled your revenge."

"The doctor will have to die for that to happen, but some jail time will do him good. Ultimately, he will be executed. When I become the President of Antarah, he will pay for the murder of my depated wife."

I stopped the tape, shaking uncontrollably. I never imagined the extent of Fouad's evil. I took a few deep breaths and tried to think before calling Brahim at the hospital.

"Our lives are in danger, we need to leave Antarah today," I said in a panic.

"What happened?" he asked.

"I have the tape. It's all here."

"Calm down, baby. Pack a light bag and meet me at the airport."

"I'm sure Fouad and Esmaa have thought of everything. Our names are probably in every checkpoint. We can't tip them off. We have to hide. What are we going to do?"

"The man at the border, Lieutenant Janoudi."

"That's right. You saved his son. I'm sure he can help us."

"I think we can trust him. Hurry Fatima, we don't have much time."

As I packed my things, I thought of everything I was leaving behind; Jamila and her unborn child, baby Ramee, Dalal, Samira, Brahim's family. I wondered if I'd ever see them again. I needed to let them know somehow about Fouad's plans to overthrow the government. They needed to be prepared for a possible civil war.

I called Jamila and briefly explained what the future might hold.

"Jamila, this might sound crazy but you have to swear by Allah that you will not call Fouad or repeat what I'm about to say."

"You are scaring me Fatima."

"Do you swear?" I asked in a sturdy voice.

"I swear by Allah."

"Fouad is planning to overthrow the government. The next few days will be chaotic. Have Samira stay with you. Call Dalal and let her know to be prepared without giving too much information. Take whatever measures you need to be safe. I love you."

"Fatima…"

I hung up.

I sensed Jamila was a bit leery of my words, and extremely concerned about my bizarre behavior. In Islam, it is forbidden to swear on anything but if you must swear you could only swear by Allah. I hated to put Jamila in that dilemma but I needed to guarantee she would keep her word and would protect the people that I loved.

As I finished packing, I came across the last camel statuette that my father had brought to me on his last trip to Antarah. On a whim, I snatched it, placing it with my clothes, passport and money. I put on my black garment that concealed my body and face.

Before meeting Brahim, I sent a letter to President Saeed by messenger explaining Fouad's intentions. I enclosed the lab results and taped conversations between Fouad and Esmaa to confirm my allegations. I made it very clear that neither Brahim nor I were involved in this sinister plan.

From taxicabs to shops to restaurants, pictures of Rauf were plastered everywhere. His presence was felt as a reminder that I owed it to him and to the people of Antarah to expose my husband for what he was: a ruthless killer.

My only hope was that the letter would reach the Presidential Palace before it was too late. Despite my resentment, it was my duty to try to redeem my father from his past mistakes and to bring closure to Rauf's family for his untimely death. I prayed for

Allah to protect our country's leader and his family and to guide them through some very challenging times.

When I arrived at the hospital, Brahim was waiting impatiently in his car.

"Fatima, get in. Thank God you're all right. Fouad was here earlier looking for you," Brahim said.

"We have to go."

I wondered if Jamila had broken her promise.

We took off and drove for over two hours. Brahim reassured me that everything would be all right, but I was very nervous. I had set in motion a volatile chain reaction. Now, there was no turning back.

"What if Fouad manages to gain control of Antarah? What then? What's going to happen to our friends and family? I couldn't live with myself if something happened to any of them."

"Fatima, your life is in eminent danger. If you stay and die, what would that accomplish? How would that help anyone?"

"I'm just so confused."

"I'm confident Lieutenant Janoudi will help us."

As we got close to the border, we noticed a lot of activity. I covered my face, afraid that someone might recognize me. Brahim went to the office to speak to the Lieutenant. Moments later, he came back.

"Are you ready? Get your things," Brahim said.

"Is everything all right?"

"As you suspected, our names are on the most wanted list in every checkpoint throughout Antarah."

"Will he help us?"

"He can only help one of us today. The office is swarming with military police. He's going to hide you in his vehicle and take you across to a nearby village. In a few days, he will do the same for me. This will give me time to look after my family; make sure they're safe. It's for the best."

"I can't go without you," I said clinging to him. "You are my life."

"Here are your bracelets. When you look at them, think of me." As he put them on my wrist he said, "This one is to remember our Mediterranean sunsets, the most beautiful moments of our lives. This one is for us never to forget the difficult times we endured away from each other. This one is my promise of the future we will build together, where nothing, not even death, will come between us. We will be reunited, Fatme. I swear, habeebtee."

At that point, I hugged him. I never wanted to let go. We kissed through the thin net that covered my face.

"I love you with all my being, ayunnee," I said.

"I love you more," he replied.

"Brahim, I have something to tell you."

At that moment, the lieutenant came up to us. He had created a distraction so I could sneak into his car unnoticed.

"We have to go now," the lieutenant shouted. "Something is happening and this might be our last chance. Doctor, I created a distraction that should give you enough time to leave this area. Goodbye and good luck."

My heart was being shredded to pieces. I was distraught because I wasn't able to tell him I was carrying his child, and that he was going to be a father. Everything happened so fast. As we began to cross the border, we heard gunfire. I looked back and a man in civilian clothes was lying on the ground. My gut told me it was Brahim. I screamed in anguish and tried to open the door to run towards him. The lieutenant held my arm. For a moment, I thought we had been set up.

"I need to go be with him," I said sobbing. "Please let me go."

"We can't go back. You would be putting both of our lives in danger. I will take you to a safe place," he said.

"I need to know what happened to Brahim," I said in a trembling voice.

"Someone must have overheard his name and checked on the list. He probably didn't make it to his car in time or tried to resist arrest. He loved you very much. I saw it in his eyes even the first time I met him. He was willing to sacrifice his life for yours."

I wept inconsolably.

"I know he'd want you to be happy and follow your heart," he said, resting his hand on my shoulder.

"Do you think he's dead? What will happen to him?"

"I don't have the answers. I just know that I owe him my son's life. If he is alive, I'll do anything I can to help him."

"When you see him, tell him I'll be waiting for him for as long as it takes. Tell him I love him," I said nervously wiping my tears, trying to convince myself everything was going to be all right.

We finally got to the village. He dropped me off at a relative's home that lived in Jordan, an hour away from the border.

"It's not much, but you'll be safe here for a while," he said.

"Thank you. Please take care of Brahim and tell him that I love him and miss him. Tell him I'll see him in a few days," I said.

As the days passed, we listened to a shortwave band radio to get news from Antarah. The family comforted me as I listened to the devastating reports that only helped me grow hopeless.

Fouad and his supporters had taken over several small towns and were threatening to use chemical weapons on the people if the president did not surrender. Bombs were going off everywhere from government administration offices and buses to public markets and museums. He was destroying anything in his path to achieve his goal.

Pictures in the Jordanian newspapers portrayed incredible destruction. A once beautiful Antarah was now surrounded by ruins. Over one hundred thousand casualties, civilian and military, had been reported. Among them were Lieutenant Janoudi and his family. I was devastated by the news. The lieutenant was a family man, a man of principles. He had risked his life for us and now, he was gone. He was also my only lifeline to Brahim. How would I ever know if he was dead or alive? I was tormented by this thought, by the uncertainty in my life, by the cruelty of my fate.

Janoudi's death was followed by some encouraging news; Fouad's days were counted. His well thought out plan had backfired. Some of his followers were infiltrators. These men were loyal to President Saeed and had a mission: to find out all the intricate details of his operation and put an end to it. Fouad and his accomplices were brought to justice and paid the ultimate price for their betrayal. Everyone involved in the coup was hung in the public plaza.

I was relieved to know that Fouad was dead and completely out of my life. It was hard to believe that I once had feelings for a man capable of such evil.

Now that the war was over, I waited patiently for Brahim. The country was still in chaos. Small anti-establishment groups had emerged, the people were looting, and the atmosphere was very unstable.

By now, my pregnancy was starting to show, so I settled in a small apartment in the village. There, with the help of a midwife, I gave birth to my precious Hasan, named after Brahim's father. I was so excited with his arrival. He was my little piece of heaven; my daily reminder of the love Brahim and I shared.

I counted the minutes, hours, days, weeks and months. There was no word from Brahim. I assumed the worst, but kept praying. I needed to believe that I would have a second chance at happiness; that my son would know his father, that I would have a family of my own.

After a year had passed, I decided to leave Jordan. I had become restless with all the coverage of the turmoil in Antarah. I needed some distance between my past and me.

I took Hasan and went to my father's Tuscan villa in Maremma. It was a magical city. The landscapes reminded me of Antarah. I understood why my father had picked this as a place to retire.

It overlooked the sea and it had an old-world feel to it. The air was fresh and the mountains were a bright green.

The view was breathtaking.

The villa wasn't our chalet in Antarah, but it shared my fondest memory: a Mediterranean sunset. As I stared into the horizon and watched the sun disappear, I dreamed that Brahim and I would once again share that moment together. I hoped that somehow we were both looking at our sunset wishing we would see it together once again.

Every day, I prayed for Brahim's safe return. Hasan would imitate my every move and repeat what I was saying. It was my obligation to educate our son with the teachings of the Qur'an and encourage prayer as an important aspect of Islam. Prayer was one of the most valuable things Brahim brought into my life.

I had brought with me the only memento I had of my father, the camel statuette. As I put it on the table, it slipped from my hands and cracked in half. While trying to glue it back together, I realized there was something in it. It was the missing piece of the puzzle, the filling in of the blanks that would bring closure to such a horrible chapter in my life.

"...the next day, I went with some high-ranking officers, who were involved in the deal, to the house of the man who masterminded this and all other past operations, Hussein Mustafa, Fouad's father.

We were demanding our cut of the pie. We were not responsible for the mishap. We did our part and we wanted our money.

Mr. Mustafa excused himself to go use the bathroom. A few minutes later, we heard a shot. He had committed suicide because he didn't have the money to pay us. He knew we would arrest him and let him rot in jail, maybe even kill him.

Now, we had a dead body and we had to come up with a credible story as to why we were in the man's house. So we explained that we got a tip about his possible connection to the drug bust and followed up with a routine inquiry visit.

The story had many holes, but no one was going to challenge my authority.

I wanted to distance myself from scandal, so I requested a new assignment. The timing was perfect. The president was ready to appoint an ambassador to the U.S. I was a trusted friend, an excellent choice.

Hussein Mustafa was survived by a wife, a son and three young daughters. Fouad's mother died shortly after his dad. His aunts and uncles helped with the household, but it wasn't enough. One day, Fouad found a letter. In it, his father gave his account of the story and mentioned my name. Fouad had the perfect weapon to blackmail me.

I sent him money on a monthly basis to help his family, I financed his military education, and even spoke to the president on his behalf.

I never suspected he was keeping close tabs on my life, especially on you. Then, that night he called me; he demanded your hand in marriage. He threatened to blow open the secrets of the past if I didn't agree.

I accepted. I admit I was a coward. I was so afraid that I would tarnish my impeccable reputation. I was a disgrace to my country, but I refused to go down after all the respect I had gained from the president and my peers. I didn't want to embarrass my family. I couldn't bare the thought of you being ashamed of me. I guess I was more of a politician than a father.

Please, never doubt my love for you. I truly thought Fouad would make you happy after all I had done for him. I rushed to so many decisions. I regret so many things. I hope you will find it in you heart to forgive me. I love you more than life itself. I wish I had sacrificed myself for your happiness. This is a mistake I will have to live with for the rest of my life."

After reading this, I had the whole story. For a few days, I was angry. Then, I realized that I couldn't change the past. I had to accept that my father wasn't perfect. Then again, who is? I paid for many of his mistakes. That was my destiny. Now, I had to let go of my hatred, forgive my father and start to heal.

I started to think of the upside of marrying Fouad which was meeting Brahim, the only man who made my life worth living. Without him, I wouldn't have my beautiful Hasan and the incomparable joy of motherhood. Everything happens for a reason, reasons we might not comprehend, reasons we might disagree with, but knowing that Allah had already written my fate, I accepted my path and hoped I could make my Creator proud of my remaining life.

Now that I was a mother, I realized we all make mistakes. I had made my share of them. As parents, we want and hope for the best for our children but sometimes it's impossible. Unintentionally, I had deprived my child of a father, of a normal life. Sometimes we don't measure the consequences of our actions.

chapter 27

Return To Antarah

Two years had passed since the day my future was shattered. I returned to a devastated Antarah. I had contributed 15 million dollars to a fund set to help rebuild a country that had been left in ruins. It was my moral obligation to assist the people of a country that I had grown to love. It was an opportunity to begin to cleanse my father's mistakes. Now was the time to face my demons and my angels.

I visited Jamila and Dalal. Ramee was already a little man and Amar, Jamila's second little boy, was a few months older than Hasan. Dalal was expecting her second child. Her daughter, Sarah, looked just like her. It was a relief to know that they were all doing fine. In the midst of chaos, there was always a glimmer of hope.

I asked Dalal about Brahim. She knew nothing. It was as if the Earth had swallowed him. I was headed for answers to Brahim's family home. I was nervous about their reaction, considering that I had put their son in harm's way, but I needed to know if they were aware of his whereabouts. First, I needed to go somewhere.

It was Friday, my last day in Antarah; a day of prayer and meditation throughout the Middle East. I remembered how Brahim and I spent Fridays at the chalet. I didn't know if I was ready to face the past, but I went anyway. I was surprised to see that the area hadn't been affected by the war. In fact, the chalet looked the same. It was there where I spoke to Hasan about his father and about how happy we were.

"Mama, why you crying?" he asked.

"I was remembering your Baba and how he loved this place. I wish you could have met him. He would have loved you so much," I said hugging and kissing him.

"Mama, mama, beach!"

We walked towards the ocean. Hasan played on the shore delighting in getting his feet wet. As I watched him splashing, I realized how much Hasan was like his father. Minutes later, I saw his sleepy eyes and I spread a blanket on the sand and put him down for a nap. He looked so peaceful. That calm just made my mind drift to the days when Brahim and I shared true happiness. I looked forward to our sunset with nostalgia.

As the sky started to display an array of vibrant colors, I heard a voice that brought me back to reality.

"Habeebtee."

I turned in disbelief.

"I prayed for this moment for the past few years," the voice continued.

"Brahim, ayunnee," I said as I tried to contain my emotions.

I couldn't believe my eyes. It was him. We ran into each other's arms as the Mediterranean sunset once again witnessed our undying love for one another. We hugged and kissed. I touched his face a million times making sure he wasn't a mirage. It was, indeed, a true miracle. Allah had not forgotten us. We didn't speak; we just lost ourselves in each other's eyes like the very first time we met. Suddenly, I felt a pull at my dress.

"Mama, who's that?" Hasan asked.

"Hasan, it's your Baba, Brahim," I replied.

"I have a son?" Brahim asked as the news brought tears to his eyes and a glow to his face with a priceless smile.

"Yes, this is Allah's blessing. Our little piece of heaven," I said.

He picked Hasan up and gave him a hug and a kiss. He looked at him with such tenderness and love.

"Mama said you love me very much," Hasan said.

"I love you more than life itself," Brahim said. "Fatme, you have made me the happiest man alive," he said as he kissed Hasan and put him down. "I wanted to do this since the day I met you. I know it seemed impossible then, but things have changed. I no longer have to hide my true feelings from the world. Believe it or not, every day I've been coming here at this time with this in my pocket hoping it would be the day I would see you again. Allah has answered my prayers."

At this moment he revealed an antique, platinum ring.

"It was my grandmother's. Before she died, she told my mother to save it for me, so that one day I could give it to my future wife. I was her favorite grandson, and I loved her with all my heart. Years later, my mom told me that the ring was lost. Right after my release from prison, my mother inexplicably came across the ring. I believed it to be a sign from Allah. You can't imagine how much hope this brought me. Here, in front of our son and this majestic sunset, I am professing my eternal love to you."

He got on one knee.

"Fatima Aziz, will you marry me?" he asked.

"Yes, ayunnee, yes," I said as I kissed his lips. "Of course, I will marry you. I've been waiting for this moment all my life," I responded with tears rolling down my cheeks while Brahim placed the ring on my finger.

"Time has passed, but my feelings for you have only deepened. I love you more than ever," he said.

As we embraced, Hasan started to clap. It was a fairy tale beginning after our tumultuous love affair.

"Mama, time to pray," Hasan said.

The three of us prayed together. We were thankful to be the family we had always dreamed of. I could tell Brahim was proud of the way I was rearing our son.

Afterwards, as I caressed Brahim's hair, I began to tell him what had happened that unfortunate day.

"As I was crossing the border, I heard the gunshot and saw you collapse. I was determined to go back for you, but Lieutenant Janoudi insisted that it would put both our lives in danger and he couldn't take that risk. I was tormented by the idea that you might be hurt, captured, tortured… and days later, when you didn't come to meet me, I feared the worst. What happened to you?"

"I was shot and left for dead. Some farmers found me and nursed me back to health. Then, I was captured and thrown in jail until the country was stabilized. One day, unexpectedly, I was released. They said it was a presidential pardon."

"I called the president to make sure he had received the letter and had cleared our names of any wrongdoing. I also inquired about your whereabouts. I explained to him that after you had helped me escape, you disappeared without a trace. I made sure he knew you had no involvement in Fouad's plot. I didn't put it past that evil man to try to frame you for his crimes," I said.

"I was nearly executed with the rest, but I guess your phone call ultimately saved me. I thought of giving up so many times, but your love was what kept me alive."

"Ayunnee, I put you through so much."

"I'd do it all over again for you, habeebtee. I came to the chalet every Friday hoping that one day I would see you again. I didn't know what to do, where to start. I thought I had lost you forever."

"You didn't. I'm not going anywhere. Our love prevailed over all the obstacles that came our way. I love you Brahim."

At that moment, we embraced and kissed each other passionately, still wondering whether it was all a dream.

After a few days, Brahim and I went to the courthouse and made our union legal. Now we were husband and wife. The following morning, the sheik came to the chalet to give us Allah's blessings.

That afternoon, we held a gathering for our friends and family to join in the celebration of our union.

Brahim wore a gilabeeah, a long tunic in white that was collarless with long sleeves and delicate white embroidery on each side.

I wore a similar white tunic with silver embroidery on the sleeve cuffs, collar, and hem. My hair was down with a simple, thin braid in the back to hold a strand of jasmine flowers.

We stood barefoot on the sand over a bed of red and white rose petals. Hasan was by our side dressed exactly like his father. It was a glorious day with a light breeze that caressed our glowing faces.

We exchanged rings just as the sun started to set. Although it wasn't customary to exchange vows, we broke tradition that day, and in front of all our guests, we expressed our deepest thoughts about one another.

"Fatme, my love, you've never looked as beautiful as you do today. It's been a long, painful journey to get here, but it has all been worth it. Seeing you here, before me, knowing that in Allah's eyes we are one, is the biggest joy of my life. To have our beautiful Hasan witnessing this day is a true gift. I thank Allah every day for bringing you and our son into my life and allowing me to love the way I love you."

"Brahim, today is the happiest day of my life. You taught me the meaning of true love. You showed me how beautiful life is when shared with someone as special as you. When Hasan was born, he filled my empty heart because I knew I had a part of you forever. Now that we've found each other again, you've made my life complete. All the sadness disappeared. I finally have the family I always dreamed of. I love you."

It was then that our guests emitted a traditional sound, zalgoota. It was similar to an American Indian war call. However, in this case, it was a joyous noise followed by well wishers' phrases for the newlyweds.

"May Allah bless your union today and forever."

"May Allah keep you healthy."

"May Allah bless you with many children."

"May Allah give you a long life and bless your lovely son."

Once again, this place had become magical. This was where we had made so many plans and promises, where we had loved each other so much. This was the place where we had found each other again and had sworn to one another eternal love, where we had looked into each others eyes and got lost in the moment; the moment when the sun and the sky become one. This was the site of our Mediterranean sunset.

It felt so right. I only wished Baba and Mama would have been there to share the happiest day of our lives. I knew someway, somehow, they were able to see the realization of what they had always wanted for me.

After an evening of food, dancing and rejoicing, Brahim's parents took Hasan to spend the night at their home. Brahim and I were alone for the first time since we reunited.

It was our first night together as husband and wife. I told Brahim I wanted to go to the guest room to prepare a surprise.

"I left you a little something on the bed," I said.

I soaked in the tub while Brahim took a shower in our room.

As I got into a red, sheer and satin gown, I could hear our Sinatra music in the background softly playing "Fly Me to the Moon." I could smell Brahim's aftershave. I felt the same excitement and anticipation as I did the first time we made love. I looked forward to seeing him in the red, satin boxers that matched my gown.

As I walked out of the room, the moonlight allowed my silhouette to be seen through my delicate gown. When I gazed at his strong, muscular body I couldn't help but thinking how handsome he looked just standing there with his radiant, flawless smile. I could tell that he was also admiring my body as I walked up to him.

When I got closer, he grabbed me by the hand and turned my body so my back was to him. Then he proceeded to caress me from the waist up. As he reached the straps of my gown, he slipped them off ever so slowly, letting my gown slide to the floor. I could feel his strong presence behind me. Then, he turned me to face him. He kissed my neck working his way up to a passionate kiss. He carried me to the bedroom. I guess he had some surprises of his own because I saw the room filled with the soft glow of candles and rose petals.

As he placed me on the bed, he whispered in my ear.

"You are so beautiful. I can't wait to make love to you all night long."

"I've been waiting for this moment all my life," I said as I whispered in his ear and nibbled it softly. "You are the only man I want, and I really want you…"

"I'm all yours, today and forever," he said, catching his breath as he kissed every part of me.

We touched and discovered our bodies all over again. We consumed each other with intensity. No force of nature could stop the deep emotions that had taken over this indescribable moment. We couldn't believe that everything we had hoped for had finally become a reality. We could love each other freely, with no guilt, no regrets, just looking forward to a future filled with hope and dreams.

"Moments like this should last forever," Brahim said.

"Moments like this have beautiful consequences."

As our energy started to deplete, we caressed and held each other with tenderness until we fell asleep.

In the morning, I found what looked like a book on my nightstand. The card read "To my habeebtee with love from ayunnee." When I looked closely, I realized that it was a journal.

"I want you to read this one day so you can grasp the depth of my love for you. It kept me sane. My most intimate and private thoughts are there for you to read. I opened my heart like I never thought possible. This isn't the time to dwell on the past. Just know that you never have to doubt my love for you."

"You could be certain that I will never take your love for granted, ayunnee."

There was a knock at the door. It was Hasan with his grandparents. It was such a touching sight.

It was difficult to say good-bye but after a few weeks, the three of us moved to the villa in Maremma to start our new life; a life away from the bittersweet memories of Antarah.

Nine months later, we were blessed with the arrival of a girl, Iman, named after my mother.

Although we visited Antarah often to see our family, friends and the site where our love blossomed, we had found peace in our Tuscan retreat.

Thankful for all our blessings, Brahim and I opened a small clinic in Maremma to take care of those less fortunate. Brahim performed pediatric surgery, free of charge, for needy families. This work was very gratifying and fulfilling on a spiritual level.

Everyday we acknowledge our good fortune and pray to Allah to watch over us. When we see our children's smiles, we can feel His presence and His immeasurable love.

When we walk out to the balcony of our villa and gaze at our Mediterranean sunset, it's inevitable to remember everything leading to this moment and to fall in love all over again. That is our beautiful gift from Allah.

Epilogue

Years later, Brahim's mom died. We were very saddened by the news, but thankful that she was able to enjoy her grandchildren. I was touched that in her final moments, she thought of me. Her last wish was for my mother's bracelet to be returned. She knew how much it meant to me. She was honored I had shared this precious family heirloom with her, and wanted me to pass it along to my own children.

This bracelet was a reminder of my beautiful childhood. It was a reminder of true love overcoming incredible obstacles. When I opened the heart, all the memories, good and bad, came flashing through. This heart had endured pain and suffering that made us stronger and an endless fountain of love that made anything possible.

As days passed, I placed two new pictures over the old ones, one of Hasan and one of Iman. This was my personal reminder to never take for granted the beautiful path Allah had traced for me and my family.

THE END

Acknowledgments

Fatima, you were my mentor, my editor, and the first person to believe in me and give me the chance to prove myself and discover my path as a writer.

Jeannette, my friend of many years, your advice and encouragement help me go on when I feel like giving up.

Elsa, an unexpected surprise, a light at the end of a tunnel. You made me believe when I thought the dream had faded. Now, it's a reality.

Adriana and Marinieves, you helped good become better.

Sally, Avery and Mark, you gave the book its final touches.

The Chaar clan: Sami and Sara the photographer and model dynamic duo, and Mohammad, a source of publishing guidance.

Last, the Mediterranean sunset photos by Morelli.

Thank you.

Yvette Canoura is a romantic suspense writer and Associated Press award-winning journalist. Born in the Bronx and raised in Puerto Rico, she earned a BA in Broadcast Journalism from Loyola University, New Orleans. She is a former newspaper writer, magazine freelancer, television and radio talk show host and member of the Southern Louisiana Chapter of Romance Writers of America.

Her fascination with the Middle East began in 1989 when she met and married her husband. Her love for his family, culture, and people inspired Mediterranean Sunset, the first in a trilogy.

LOUISIANA AUTHOR PROJECT
2019 Adult Fiction Winner